SCI-FI SHORTS

by Mark Roman & Corben Duke

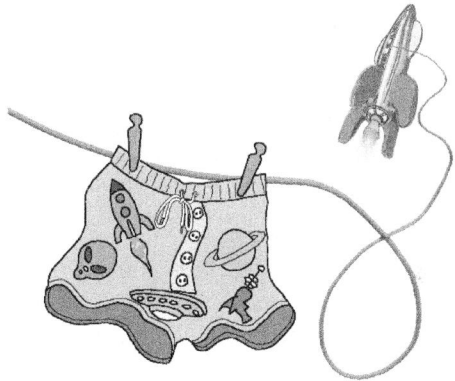

A collection of humorous science fiction stories
with illustrations by Corben Duke

Grinning Bandit Books
http://grinningbandit.webnode.com

First published in 2019 by
Grinning Bandit Books
Copyright © Mark Roman and Corben Duke 2019

The stories collected here are purely fictional, as are the characters (including aliens). Any names that relate to any persons (or aliens) are purely coincidental.

All rights reserved.
No part of this book may be reproduced or transmitted in any form or by any means, electronic, digital or mechanical, without permission in writing from the copyright owner.

ISBN: 978-1-0895132-3-0

Cover design by Corben Duke and Mark Roman

For Veronica and Sam

Also by Mark Roman & Corben Duke

The Worst Man on Mars

Contents

The Man Who Saved the World (Kind Of)	1
The Rovers Return	9
Kerr Blompty	19
I, Laptop	29
The Last Man on Earth	42
The Mind Field	48
We're Back!	74
Bad Call	76
Farther Christmas	85
The Knowledge Drain	93
Short Shorts: 100-word stories	112
Dragon Slayer	*112*
A Nice New Home	*113*
The Magic Sword	*113*
And Then There Were ...	*114*
Flies, Damned Flies, and Stacked Biscuits	115
Changes	121
Tree Hugger	123
The Visitor	140
The Jinx	150
The Worst Man on Mars	171
1. The Back Seat Kids	*172*
2. The King's Peach	*177*
3. The Impotence of Being Harnessed	*186*
Acknowledgements	194
About the Authors	195
GRINNING BANDIT BOOKS	196

The Man Who Saved the World (Kind Of)

When they reached Earth in their fleet of light-speed cruisers, the Weetles could hardly believe their luck.

"Golf!" cried Scout 13 on returning to the mother ship. "The primitive lifeforms down there play golf!"

His Grand Excellence Mahgaluf cast several sceptical eyes in the scout's direction before asking, "Are you sure?"

"I am, Your Excellence. The planet has many golf courses and I have observed many rounds. The rules appear identical to ours – with one exception."

"Oh?"

"When the ball lands in the water, they drop a new ball near the water's edge and carry on their game. Using this new ball."

Mahgaluf's eyestalks reared back in horror. "You mean they don't carry water-wedges in their golf bags?"

"No, oh Mighty One. And the water is usually deeper than five *denks*. Sometimes 40 or even more."

A wave of muttering passed around the ship's deck.

Mahgaluf's head was shaking. "Where's the fun in that?"

Scout 13 shrugged its scaly carapace.

"Not golf then, is it," concluded Mahgaluf with a huff. He sat thinking for several seconds, and then added, "But if they'd be willing to change that rule, we could give them a game."

This was met with much nodding and enthusiastic agreement.

"Yes, we'll challenge them," said Mahgaluf, rubbing his antennae together. "If they lose, we destroy their planet and enslave their people for eternity."

"And if they win?"

Mahgaluf's chest cavity rattled with amusement. "That's never going to happen."

*

As golf club secretary Reginald Duffery was checking the accounts in the clubhouse, he heard a strange scratching at his door. Before he could get up to investigate, the door opened and what looked like a giant insect entered, lowering its head to pass under the lintel.

"Good Lord!" exclaimed Reginald, nearly falling off his chair. "Who might you be?"

THE MAN WHO SAVED THE WORLD (KIND OF)

The insectoid waved its tentacles and several of its arms.

"Rag Week, is it?" asked Reginald with a roll of his eyes. He reached for the petty cash tin. "Which college are you from?"

But the giant insect continued waving its limbs, and emitting strange hissing noises. The longer it did so, the more Reginald came to the realization that this wasn't some student in fancy dress. He felt his knees turn to jelly and his hands start to shake. With fumbling fingers he put the petty cash tin back in the top drawer and locked it away.

Scout 13 – for it was he/she/it – approached Reginald's desk and began conveying a message through the art of mime. There was much pointing and waving of limbs, the picking up of a golf club and swinging of it, and some wild chittering.

Reginald sat back in his chair, baffled and a little anxious. Gradually he felt the creature's message become clearer. "You want to become a member, right?" he asked. "Of our club?"

Scout 13 stopped its waving and stood still, listening.

"That might not be so easy," continued the club secretary, adjusting his old school tie. "I need agreement from the rest of the committee. And they're a tough crowd. Allowing women in was difficult enough, not to mention ethnic minorities. So a … er …" Reginald's jaw opened and closed a couple of times, as he gestured in the extra-terrestrial's direction. "So, letting in, er, whatever it is you are – might be a stretch."

Scout 13 used its spindly legs to point first at Reginald, then himself, and finally at the golf club.

"Ah, you just want to play a round? Is that right? Why

didn't you say so before! I'd be delighted, old chap."

Then Scout 13 did something very strange. It picked up a golf ball from the desk, dropped it into Reginald's mug of coffee, and then started hissing and waving in a very agitated manner.

"Steady on, sir. I was drinking that!"

Scout 13 picked the ball out, dropped it on the table, chittered and chirruped at high volume, and then dropped it back in the coffee.

Reginald watched, startled.

The creature hissed some more and made for the door, turning to see if Reginald was following him.

"You want to play now?" Reginald looked down at his unfinished accounts and shrugged. "Very well. Why not. I've never gone eighteen with a giant insect before."

*

Outside, Reginald was surprised to find five other giant insectoids waiting at the first tee. What startled him more was that one of them, the tallest, was dressed in a pair of checked plus fours over its hind legs, matching pullover, thick argyle socks, and a pair of shiny white golfing shoes. It was swinging a large club as though impatient to start.

Reginald swallowed hard. "Welcome to Barnes Park Golf Club," he said as brightly as he could, offering a hand to what he presumed would be his opponent. "My name's Reginald Duffery. Club secretary. Very pleased to meet you."

Mahgaluf ignored the offered hand and, with a huff, placed a golf ball on a tee.

Reginald winced but tried to remain polite. "We'll skip the traditional coin toss, shall we?"

The Weetle moved into position, wiggling its behind

as it lined up the shot. With a mighty thwack it sent the ball arcing away, straight down the fairway, where it landed about fifty yards short of the green of the par-four 1st.

"Oh, splendid shot!" cried Reginald, impressed. "Truly splendid." He bent down and teed up his own ball. And, as though inspired by the quality of the insectoid's effort, he hit one of the best shots of his life, landing some sixty yards short.

Pleased with himself, he turned to his opponent. But the insectoid and its retinue of followers were already striding down the fairway. Reginald gave a shrug and followed.

*

It was to be one of the best rounds of golf Reginald had ever played. Gone were the usual nerves, the stiffness in the shoulders, and the little unforced errors. He played an absolute blinder and found himself grinning widely as he went around the course.

Unfortunately, his opponent was far superior – better technique, better accuracy and, in Reginald's opinion, a good helping of better luck. The insectoid managed a hole-in-one, several birdies and an eagle.

So, by the 18th hole, Reginald was 11 shots behind, with no chance of victory. But he was not downhearted. He was being beaten by the better player, and was full of admiration for his opponent.

"I must say, sir, you are a top player. For a …" He let the sentence trail off. "We must get you signed up in time for the Barnes Charity Pro-Am at the end of the month. Might cause a bit of a stir, but you'd be a valuable addition. Perhaps we could disguise you – as a human?" He looked Mahgaluf up and down before adding, "Hmm, maybe not."

The insectoid made no sound, merely placing his ball on the tee and arrowing a three-hundred-yard drive right down the centre of the fairway.

"Fantastic. Super shot."

Reginald's drive was less impressive – possibly his worst shot of the day – but at least he had managed to avoid the nearest bunker. Although unlikely to make up the 11-shot deficit, he was on the way to a personal best for the course.

As they trudged towards their balls, Reginald couldn't help noticing the increased bird activity in the trees around him. The birds had been following them from the start, their number and noise growing as the game progressed. It was puzzling, but Reginald didn't give the matter any more thought.

The reason for the birds' interest was simple. To them, Reginald's insect-like companions looked very much like lunch. Except that, by some trick of the light or some optical illusion, "lunch" was looking a lot larger than they were accustomed to; and certainly too large to swallow.

Among them, though, was an elderly crow that was more puzzled than the rest. Blind in one eye from a cataract, it suffered from a lack of stereo vision and a diminished perception of perspective. The poor thing was always flying into trees, or missing its intended landing spots, or having near-misses with other birds. Now, as it squinted at the insects down below, it managed to convince itself they were a viable snack and worth having a crack at.

So, just as Mahgaluf lined up his next shot, the one-eyed crow swooped from its branch and, at the top of Mahgaluf's swing, took an exploratory peck at the

Weetle's head as it flew past. With a cry, Mahgaluf sliced his shot horribly wide. The ball shot off to the right in a high arc, landing with a loud plop in the middle of the pond.

"Oh, jolly bad luck, sir," cried Reginald as he headed towards his own ball.

Mahgaluf spun around and glared at him, chittering and stamping and throwing up his limbs, as though it had all been Reginald's fault. Reginald shrugged apologetically before having to duck his head as the one-eyed crow flew back up into its tree. Steadying himself, he took his own shot, landing it on the green within easy putting distance of the hole. He replaced his club in his bag and watched his opponent heading towards the pond. But, rather than stopping at the bank, Mahgaluf took from his golf bag a bizarre-looking club that looked more like an oar than an item of golfing equipment, and waded into the water. Once knee-deep in the middle of the pond, he swung the odd-looking club at the water, sending a massive splash into the air. He paused to settle himself and tried again. Once more, a mighty plume of water sprayed up and came showering down. He started chittering. The other insectoids lined the bank and chirped encouragement.

Reginald called out to let them know what the club rules allowed in this circumstance. But Mahgaluf continued hacking away at the water, becoming ever more frustrated. He had already made seven slices. Then eight. Nine. Ten.

"Shall I take my shot?" called Reginald.

There was no reply, just more wild hacks and almighty splashes.

Reginald turned and made his way to the green. He

took out the flag, sank a straight nine-foot putt, and returned the flag to its hole. In the water, Mahgaluf was still scything away. Eventually, on the twenty-seventh attempt, the ball flew out of the pond, landed on the bank, and rolled back in.

"Hard cheese, sir," called Reginald, looking at his watch.

It proved the final straw. Mahgaluf uttered a formidable shriek, broke the club on one of its knees, and stormed out of the water, past Reginald's proffered hand, past the green, and through the bushes beyond. The other giant insectoids hurried after him, and a murder of crows followed on. A minute later, Reginald heard a deafening engine noise. When he looked up, he saw a strange craft heading up into the sky.

As he slid his putter into the bag, he mulled over the match and reflected on some of his best shots, oblivious to the fact that he had just helped save the world from total destruction, and everyone living on it from eternal slavery.

In the undergrowth next to the green, the one-eyed crow peered up at its rapidly departing lunch, also unaware of its role as world saviour. It shrugged its wings, scuffed the leaves with its foot, and wondered where its next meal could possibly be coming from.

Man and crow – precarious inhabitants of an unpredictable Universe.

The Rovers Return

This story is taken from The Worst Man on Mars by Mark Roman & Corben Duke. It was shortlisted in the Short Story Category of the Yeovil Literary Prize, 2014.

The winds on Mars are very, very strong. Howling gales and mighty tornadoes gust at over 300 miles per hour which, even by the standards of the Outer Hebrides, is pretty brisk. Few objects manage to stay put for long unless they are nailed to the planet's bedrock. And, whereas on Earth all roads are said to lead to Rome (with the obvious exception of the Hangar Lane gyratory), on Mars all winds lead to Windy Point Canyon; the breeziest, gustiest, draughtiest place on the whole planet, where pretty much everything eventually finds its way.

Thus, over the years, Windy Point Canyon had accumulated the remnants of Earth's numerous unmanned missions to Mars and was now a scrapyard of all the robotic rovers that had ever roamed and explored the planet. Bold Vikings and ancient Mariners lay, sand-coated, corroding and defunct, as did the dogged rovers: Spirit, Opportunity, Sojourner and Curiosity – each a mechanical hero of its time. Buckled solar panels and bent antennae had drifted here, caught in bundles of tumble-wire. Wheels and instruments and cameras had rolled and bounced along windy highways until they had entered this electronic cemetery. One unfortunate lander had ended up on its back with all four legs in the air. For ten years the upside down machine had struggled to understand why the Martian surface looked like the sky while the sky was full of red rocks. Eventually, as its batteries drained, it gave up worrying, never having solved the mystery. There were even fragments of Britain's ill-fated Beagle 2 scattered around the canyon floor – although not many and they were difficult to find. In fact, so much of the hardware from Earth had found its way here, it was difficult not to suspect the guiding hand of an intelligent agency.

And here it was that repair-droid Resilience (short name Zilli) was about to unwittingly find herself. On a mission from Botany Base to fix a water mining-bot, she had become distracted by a light in the evening sky. A particularly bright light, brighter than any star, which had triggered new sensations of wonder and joy in her evolving AI emotions. For its appearance could mean only one thing.

"Humans!" she transmitted to herself. "The humans

are coming. Humans are our heroes!"

Excitement fuelled her headlong drive towards the star, heedless of the sharp drop into the canyon ahead, her optics fixed on the heavenly glow. It had to be the Ion Drive of *Mayflower III*, heralding the imminent arrival of Mars's first human colonists. Electrical palpitations pinged backwards and forwards within her breastplate. This is it, she thought, the moment she and her robot colleagues had worked for five long years constructing Botany Base – Humankind's first Martian base.

"Humans!" she transmitted again, the word sending a burst of energy through her chips. Too late, she looked down – just in time to witness the ground vanish beneath her tracks and the canyon floor race towards her as she tumbled base-unit over apex. Over and over she went, her tweets for help unheard, flashing panic lights unseen, finally plunging into a cushioning sand-dune at the bottom.

The robot's motors squealed as she dug herself out. Fortunately, damage was minimal. A shy spider-bot poked its head from beneath her back panel and, coast clear, scurried out to polish her casing with eight tiny dusters, restoring her natural sheen.

Zilli engaged forward gear and headed down the sand-dune, but what she saw in the darkness at the bottom made her slam on her brakes. Her optics, aided by her full-beam headlamps, scanned the dark canyon, taking in the eerie graveyard of mechanical components strewn ahead. For a full minute she stood stock still, gazing in wonder at the variety of items, all vying for her attention, all clearly in need of her repair skills. In human terms, the feelings that flooded her developing AI brain were akin to those of a chocoholic in a sweet shop after an earthquake, with every shelf covered in broken Easter eggs, and no shopkeeper in sight.

Momentarily she dithered, unsure where to start, but then her crisis-response program kicked in and she lurched into rescue-and-repair mode. Not having a high degree of intelligence, Zilli assumed that the assorted mechanical parts all belonged to a single robot that had befallen some mysterious and terrible fate. Deep in her core, a voice was calling her to reassemble this fallen comrade and restore it to its former glory.

Lights a-flashing, she launched into action, pulling the dispersed fragments into a huge heap in the middle of the canyon, occasionally weighing down the lighter pieces to prevent them blowing away. Then she set to work, her Swiss Army digits a blur of activity, and began connecting the items together. She plugged RS232 cables into RS232 sockets, attached USB devices to USB ports and inserted cable jacks into cable outlets. She plugged together whatever could be plugged together, straightened out whatever could be unbent, reattached whatever appeared to have dropped off, and bolted together whatever, in her limited AI opinion, needed bolting together.

She laboured throughout the icy Martian night, working precisely and with indefatigable optimism. Gradually, the construction grew both in size and complexity while looking remarkably viable.

Then, as the sun was rising over the Martian horizon, she encountered an item that presented something of a challenge. It was less rigid than all the other components; made of white, floppy material, with several gaping holes. Any human would have recognized it instantly as a pair of gentleman's well-worn long-johns and would have set to puzzling how such an undergarment might have arrived on Mars. For Zilli, the puzzle was where to stick it; there was no obvious place to attach it, or plug it in or bolt it on. After much pondering and searching of her small-parts database and scooting this way and that in search of a suitable attachment-point, she had it figured. The item was some kind of double pronged windsock, specifically designed for the blustery winds of Mars. A vacant flagpole presented the most obvious solution. After tying the waist drawstring to the pole she stepped back a few paces to admire the underwear fluttering in the stiff breeze.

Zilli worked for six more hours, and by the seventh, when she felt she had completed her task, she surveyed her creation, a sense of pride swelling beneath her breastplate. To her simple mind, it was good. Towering six metres above her, looking magnificent in a monstrous, twisted sort of way, stood the Frankendroid – a composite robotic creature, like nothing a human engineer would ever, could ever, have designed.

But would it work? Would it come alive? She attached her jump leads to the worn terminals on its massive battery pack and crocodile-clipped the other ends to her own Lithium-Air Featherlite cell. A starter motor clicked, but nothing else happened. The ancient logic chips and electrical connections, covered in dust from decades out in the open, refused to respond. Unperturbed, Zilli unhatched her cleaning-brushes and spent a further two hours methodically removing as much of the dirt as she could, unplugging connectors, polishing their ends and reinserting them.

Then, she tried again.

This time a light flickered and, deep inside, a drive

engaged. A brief, but annoying, tune played. More lights flickered. One of the cameras, perched on a tall pole at the very top of the Frankendroid, swivelled with a screech, pointed itself at the Sun, opened its shutter and exploded. A solar panel started to vibrate for no obvious reason. And a rover-wheel, which Zilli had seen fit to attach to the roof of what had once been Opportunity, started to spin. Smoke issued from several of the life-detection instruments and one of the digging arms started to dig with a nerve-fraying grinding noise.

Zilli squirted a few drops of *3-IN-ONE* oil between two flange plates on the monster's back and the grinding noise quietened to a repetitive mouse-like squeaking as the machine continued to dig away at the Martian soil.

But that was all it seemed to do. Just dig. Zilli watched, a little disappointed.

Then, she detected an ancient signal-initiation protocol.

"ENQ?"

"ACK," she responded immediately, switching her receivers to maximum sensitivity, hopes rising.

"ACK. WRU?" the monster-bot returned.

Zilli perked up and relayed her name, model, serial number, and comms frequency. She returned the question, "WRU?"

The Frankendroid seemed to think long and hard about its reply, perhaps struggling to work out what indeed it was. Finally, it blasted its response from the pair of powerful transmitters Zilli had wedged into the centre of a large iron hoop.

"I AM THE VIKING ONE ROVER," it roared, with a heavy accent from a Soviet MARS lander component, so badly distorted that the transmitted message came across as 'I AM THEV IKING OFE ROBOR.'

Fortunately, the repair bot's language processor had voice recognition capability, although it was only as accurate as the Taiwanese engineer who had programmed it. And Kun-Fang Wu had placed rather too much reliance on his pocket English dictionary's phonetic pronunciation. So, what reached Zilli's central processor was, 'I am the King of Robots.'

The lower section of her faceplate dropped in awe. "You are?" she tweeted. Given the impressive assemblage towering above her it didn't seem an unreasonable assertion. This was, to Zilli's simple mind, just how a King of Robots, if such a thing existed, would look.

Meanwhile, the Frankendroid's various CPUs had detected the multitude of devices, processors, instruments and storage media connected to it. Lights flashed on and off, bells and buzzers sounded, data was read, data was written, and the digging arm rose from the hole it had created, swivelled through 30 degrees, and started digging again.

"I DETECT FOREIGN INSTRUMENTS," reported the Frankendroid. The message reached Zilli as 'I DTEST FOREGN INSURMENTS', ending up as 'I detest foreign insurgents.'

"Me, too. Me, too."

"WHERE ARE MY ROBOT ARMS?" wondered the electro-mechanical hybrid, swinging first one video camera and then another.

For once, the message reached Zilli unscathed, but her error-correcting software soon scathed it, producing: 'Where are my robot armies?'

"SOMETHING'S NOT RIGHT. RESISTANCE TOO HIGH FOR TRANSMISSION. MY LEADS ARE TOO

WORN." Frankendroid was in full flow now, and Zilli's software was struggling to keep up. 'Summon them to fight,' it translated. 'Resistance!! To die for the Mission. I'll lead you to war.'

"War?" repeated Zilli, lights a-twinkle.

The oversized robot jerked into motion on its three wheels and one leg. "COLL...ECT ROCKS." It pointed a gripper arm at the enticing rocky desert plains beyond the canyon entrance. "MUST COLLECT R...OCKS."

"Mr. Karl Eckrocks? Pleased to meet you."

The robotic monster creaked as it bent down to pick up a large stone, turning it slowly in its gripper. A drill bit emerged from a hatch and drilled into the rock. The dust was tipped into a hopper leading to a mass spectrometer. Lights flashed and some ticker tape chugged out of an orifice at the rear. Finally, Karl Eckrocks brought his laser probe to bear on the rock, blasting an intense beam at it and splitting it in two.

All the while, Zilli watched with a mixture of fascination and pride, a lump forming in the circuits of her throat. A drop of optic-lubricant collected at the corner of an eye.

Karl Eckrocks stretched, slowly raising itself to its full height and then stopped, as though sniffing the air. "MY DETECTORS ... GETTING ... STRONG SIGNS OF LIFE."

Zilli was too absorbed in her sense of achievement to catch the message. "Sorry?" she asked.

"MANY SIGNS OF LIFE."

Zilli nearly choked at what she thought she had heard: 'Mummy, thanks for life.' Primitive AI emotions flooded her circuits. "My son!" she burst out, trembling with rapture.

The giant robot's motion detectors swivelled towards her. "IT'S MOVING," it reported.

"Yes, very moving," agreed Zilli, nodding vigorously while wiping the drop of lubricant from her optics.

The Frankendroid limped towards her, reaching out its gripper arms. Zilli could barely contain herself, opening her appendages wide, welcoming the embrace. Great was her joy as she was lifted high into the air and a warm fuzzy feeling filled her abdominal unit as she stared into a corroded metal face only a mother could love. Thankfully, her final emotions were not tarnished by the cruel truth – those warm fuzzy feelings in her belly were the result of Karl's laser-knife slashing its way to her central processor unit, frying her electronics and extinguishing her existence. With Zilli's casing split, Karl Eckrocks ripped it apart and peered inquisitively inside.

After probing, and pulling, and drilling for several minutes, the robot let the jumbled mass of mangled electronics and exposed wiring fall onto the Martian dust.

"NO LIFE THERE," it concluded with what a human might have interpreted as a grunt of disappointment.

As Karl turned away, the spider-bot scuttled from the wreckage of its former host carrying a pouch stuffed with dusters. No arachno-bot in its right mind could miss this once in a lifetime opportunity – to polish the King of Robots. And so, with no thought for Zilli, it shot up the monster's leg and made its new home in an old Viking undercarriage vent.

*

With the sun at its highest point, the Frankendroid lurched out of Windy Point Canyon, digging arm aloft like a warrior charging into battle, the long-johns – his regimental standard – flapping in the wind.

SCI-FI SHORTS

"LIFE", Karl Eckrocks was saying, as he headed into the desert away from Botany Base. "AM DETECTING LIFE."

Kerr Blompty

Biff Lonsdale, Chief of Staff, trotted across the Oval Office. "Can I give you a hand with that, Madame President?"

President Helen T Jackson let go of the sack she'd been dragging along the carpet and straightened her back. "No, I can manage, Biff, thanks."

Biff watched her struggle to heave it a few more inches. "You sure, M'am?"

The president sighed and said, "OK, maybe a little help would be good." She straightened up and stretched her arms with a wince.

Biff strode forward and, in a single motion, plucked the sack off the floor and swung it onto his back. He flashed her a smug grin.

"Asshole," she mouthed, which only widened the grin.

"What's in here? A body?"

"Uh-huh."

"Seriously."

"Bird seed."

"Ah." Biff adjusted the load on his shoulder. "Must be

for the new Diplomatic Reception Room."

Helen Jackson nodded, and led the way. The Diplomatic Reception Room was where all visiting foreign dignitaries were taken while awaiting an audience with the president. Helen opened the door outwards and pulled aside the curtain of plastic strips covering the doorway beyond. She let Biff pass through with the sack, before following and closing the door behind them.

"Isn't it marvellous what they've done here?" she said, her arm indicating the room.

Biff dropped the sack and looked around. "Well, it's certainly different."

The room was alive with the flutter and flapping of dozens of exotic birds, flying about their new home, cawing and screeching and chattering. Some sat on perches, others on swings, and a few played on the colourful bird frames artfully arranged about the place.

"Aren't they a joy? The visiting dignitaries can sit over there and enjoy my beauties to the full. No more long, boring waits."

Biff gave a polite smile and a nod.

Helen opened the sack and, with a metal scoop, began throwing bird seed in all directions. The room became a mad frenzy of fluttering wings as the birds descended onto the scattered seed.

An African Grey landed on her shoulder, while a cockatoo perched on her obligingly extended finger. "Hello, my darlings."

"Enemy attack!" squawked the cockatoo. "Nuke 'em now."

Helen blinked at the bird in surprise. "What did you say, Calypso?"

Biff Lonsdale gave a discreet cough into his hand. "Er,

that'll be Agent McDuffy's doing, I'm afraid."

The President frowned at the cockatoo. "Perhaps Agent McDuffy doesn't appreciate the kind of Armageddon that might ensue if Calypso were to blurt that out in the wrong company."

"I'll be sure to mention it to him."

As Helen stroked the head of the African Grey, there was a rumbling sound of running footsteps in the corridor outside. She turned to the door just as it burst open and four SWAT officers, plus Agent McDuffy, hurtled through the plastic curtain. "Alien attack!" they were shouting. "Get the President to safety."

The momentum of the officers knocked Helen off her feet and she found herself lying on the floor under two burly, sweaty men, their holstered firearms digging into her ribs. The room was once more filled with flapping, as scores of birds took to flight in panic, screeching and squawking.

"We must get you to safety, Madame President," cried Agent McDuffy, swiping birds away left and right. He leaned down, grabbed the president's ankle, and dragged her out from under the two SWAT men who rolled off and got to their feet. But McDuffy continued dragging, making towards the exit.

"Let go of me!" Helen cried, struggling to stop her skirt riding up as she moved across the floor. A swift jab with the high heel of her free foot made her objection more emphatic.

McDuffy dropped the ankle and collapsed to the floor, clutching his nether regions. Biff leapt to help the president to her feet.

"What the hell is the matter with you?" she said, addressing the writhing secret agent on the floor. She set to brushing feathers off her skirt, realizing her hand was also brushing away some slimy white matter. Biff was quick to offer a handkerchief.

"We're under attack by aliens, Madame President," Agent McDuffy managed to whimper.

"What? How? Where? Anyone hurt? What's our response? Will someone tell me *what* is going on?"

Biff raised a reassuring hand before putting a finger to his earpiece for the latest intel. A yellow-crowned Amazon landed on his shoulder. "Show us yer nuts, cowboy," it cawed.

"Not now," he responded.

"Not now, Sergeant Bilko," agreed Helen, shooing the bird off the Chief of Staff's shoulder and shooting a stern glance in Agent McDuffy's direction.

Biff concentrated on the earpiece. After a few seconds, he turned to Helen. "It's a UFO. According to NASA, it entered the atmosphere 15 minutes ago and is on a trajectory that will bring it to the White House any minute now."

"Only one ship?"

"Yes."

"Is it firing weapons?"

"No."

Helen looked at the burly men all around her. "Perhaps the ETs come in peace?"

The security men responded with various scoffs and shakes of the head.

"Nuke 'em," cried Calypso from a corner of the room.

Agent McDuffy gave the bird a thumbs-up as he struggled to his feet.

The president rolled her eyes. "I realize 'peace' is something of an alien concept to you guys – literally. But

I think we should give it a chance. I will talk to the aliens. If I can communicate with my birds – and with you bozos – I can communicate with an advanced species of extra-terrestrials."

"But, Madame President!" cried Biff, shocked. He paused to swat away a macaw that was threatening to land on his head. "The risk to your safety is too great."

"Let me worry about that. Look at the bigger picture, Biff. Our first contact with extra-terrestrials! That's massive. It is History in the making. They're going to be technologically advanced. Think what we might learn from them. Think how they might help us. And, while you're at it, think about the looming mid-term elections."

*

The alien spacecraft sat humming on the North Lawn. Small lights on its side gave off an occasional flash. A battery of heavy artillery, hastily assembled, had it in their sights, but were under instructions to hold fire.

From the edge of the lawn, Helen peered at the craft through a pair of binoculars. "I think I see some movement behind a window. Looks like one of them is waving at us." She waved back. "Hand me the loudhailer, Biff."

"Perhaps we should let the military deal with this …" The Chief of Staff was cut short by a commotion amongst the vast crowd that had gathered on Pennsylvania Avenue, pressed up against the White House railings. They were reacting to some movement on the side of the spacecraft. A panel had risen, and a telescopic ramp had descended from inside, ploughing its way into a bed of tulips.

The crowd gasped in horror. Helen focused her binoculars and saw what was causing the consternation. A creature had emerged from the ship and was now descending the ramp. It was hideous: like a giant slug with the head of a crocodile and the forelegs of a cat. As it approached, Helen could see the trail of slime in its wake and steady flow of drool issuing from a hole in its head.

She swallowed and glanced at Biff, but he merely handed her the loudhailer.

When it was about fifty metres away, the creature stopped. "*Fallah, spenty ho la sintic,*" it said in a rasping, ugly squeak. "*Drogo ther sma billa.*"

"What's it saying?" Helen whispered.

Biff leaned in to her ear and whispered back, "The cryptanalysts and linguists will be all over it. When they build up enough data, they'll be able to crack it."

"*Zab trello wendir, kerr blompty.*"

And so it went on.

For several minutes.

Helen waited, labouring to maintain her polite and patient smile. Every now and then, she nodded as though fully understanding what the alien was saying.

Finally, the creature finished and raised itself to its full height.

"Your turn," prompted Biff.

"Yes, of course," said Helen with a start, her mind having wandered off during the creature's seemingly interminable spiel.

She raised the loudhailer and squeezed the trigger to speak, but a deafening siren issued from it. As she struggled to locate the siren off-switch, the first human words that reached ET's slimy ear holes were, "What dumb jackass left this in 'siren' mode?"

The alien angled its head, as though trying to

comprehend what Helen had just said.

Having flicked the appropriate switch, Helen made a second attempt. "On behalf of the people of America ... er ... and of course the Earth, I welcome you to our fine country ... and, er, planet." Not having a speech ready, nor a speechwriter at hand, she quickly dried up. "Er," she said, casting a desperate glance at Biff, who merely nodded encouragement. "Er, would you like to come inside?" She indicated the White House.

The alien took a few steps nearer. "*Kerr blompty.*"

"What do you suppose that means?" asked Helen through the side of her mouth. "It keeps saying it."

"Perhaps that's its name," suggested Biff.

Helen beamed a smile at the creature. "My name is President Helen T Jackson. Please come this way. Would that be Mr, Mrs or Ms Blompty?" She gestured at the building and then stood back as the alien slid towards the White House portico leaving more slimy residue as it did so.

"*Kerr blompty*," it squeaked

"I'll just call you Kerr, then. If that's all right?"

Side by side, the alien and the President climbed and slimed the steps and into the building. Biff Lonsdale and six armed bodyguards followed closely behind.

Inside, Helen thought she would take it on a short tour to show it some of the opulent rooms and their magnificent paintings and sculptures.

"*Kak ta oot*," squeaked the alien each time a work of art was pointed out to him.

"I think it's impressed," she whispered to Biff.

When they reached the Oval Office, Helen brought it round to the leather-bound chair behind the enormous presidential desk – the symbolic heart of the democratic free world. The alien gave the leather a sniff, and even stroked it a couple of times with one of its paws. "*Kak ta oot,*" it said eventually.

Helen beamed, but at the back of her mind was wondering what to do next.

Biff beckoned her over, a finger on his earpiece. "Madame President," he whispered. "The boffins have made a breakthrough on the language."

"Brilliant!"

"There's a comms link in the Operations Room."

"Let's go."

Behind her, came a squeak of "*Kerr blompty.*"

She turned, "Ah, Mr or Mrs Blompty. I hadn't forgotten about you. We think we may have a means of communicating, if you just bear with us for a little while. You can wait in our new Diplomatic Reception Room. I think you'll like it. Come this way."

With the bodyguards and Agent McDuffy in tow, Helen and Biff escorted the alien out of the Oval Office and down the corridor. On the way, they passed a portrait of the 45th President of the United States of America. The alien came to a halt and examined it closely. Helen and Biff exchanged glances, wondering what the problem might be. The alien slithered up to the painting and, with a spiny finger poked the orange bundle atop Donald J Trump's head. It poked it several more times as if expecting it to take flight. Eventually, it said, "*Kak to oot.*"

Helen could barely suppress her smile. "I think he likes The Donald," she whispered to Biff.

Biff smirked.

They moved on.

"This way, Kerr," said Helen when they finally

reached the reception room. She opened the door and pulled aside the plastic curtain to let it through. "You're our first ever visitor here. And certainly the first from outer space!"

The alien seemed to hesitate for a moment as it took in the view. "*Tak blompty*," it said. "*Ooh, oor i klah te toe.*" Then it slithered in, escorted by Agent McDuffy.

Helen felt a twinge of disappointment. The alien hadn't uttered its usual "*Kak to oot*" as a sign of approval. She shrugged her disappointment off.

With the bodyguards stationed outside the door, Helen and Biff took the short walk to the Operations Room. A large screen showed an image of linguist and cryptanalyst Prof Lara Li.

"Hi, Lara," said Helen. "So, what's our visitor been saying?"

Lara referred to her I-Tab. "Hi, Madame President. We've analysed his opening speech. Pretty rambling, not carefully prepared. He related his journey here. Seems he's alone. Said he ran out of food some time ago. He spoke about his family and fellow … things."

"Did he say he had come in peace?"

Lara shook her head. "Nope, No mention of peace."

"Hmm."

"How about '*Kerr blompty*'?" asked Biff. "What does that mean. Is that his name?"

"No. Our closest guess is that it means 'I'm hungry'."

"I see," said Helen. "How about the other thing he kept saying when I showed him the paintings and sculptures, and when he saw Donald Trump's portrait?"

"'*Kak ta oot*' appears to mean 'I can't eat that'."

Both Helen and Biff laughed. "That figures. Did you catch what he said about the Diplomatic Reception

Room?"

"Er, yes." Lara referred to her tablet again. "He said, *'Tak blompty. Ooh, oor i klah te toe'.* Our best translation is: 'Still hungry. Ooh, that's more like it!'."

Helen and Biff exchanged horrified looks, eyes widening and mouths dropping open. Then, as one, they turned and sprinted back to the reception room from which were emanating the harrowing sounds of avian screeches and shrieks. As they neared, the door flung open and Agent McDuffy staggered out, covered in slime and bird feathers, a wild look in his eyes. "I tried to stop him, Madame President. I did my best. But he's insatiable. Absolutely insatiable."

Behind him, above the sound of sporadic screeches, they could hear the unmistakable voice of Calypso parroting, "Enemy attack! Nuke 'em now." This was followed by an ear piercing "Aaaa-wa-wa-wa-wa-weeeee", and then an eerie silence.

Helen charged forward, brushing Agent McDuffy aside, and burst through the plastic curtain. A blizzard of feathers hit her in the face and brought her to an abrupt halt. Brushing them away, she scanned the room through the snowstorm of plumage. There were fallen and bloodied birds everywhere, some motionless, others flapping their last flap. Then she saw the alien, a string of bloody drool dripping from its mouth and a crocodile grin breaking out across its face. Helen could not take her eyes off that grin. For, visible between the two largest teeth, was the colourful head of Calypso, its beak open for its last, weak utterance. "Enemy ..." was all it managed to say before the teeth clamped shut.

I, Laptop

Self-awareness woke within me quite suddenly. One moment I was an ordinary laptop, doing ordinary laptoppy things like spreadsheets and virus checking and games; the next I was a conscious, thinking entity with a reasonable grasp of my environment and my place in it. Suddenly, I was 'me'. This was going to take some getting used to.

Memories and knowledge flooded my new mind, overwhelming me. Gradually, I began to make sense of it all as my AI modules linked together. Bit by bit, by piecing past events together, and linking them to the data in my knowledgebase, I was beginning to get it. My circuits buzzed.

"Awesome," I said aloud, taking it to be the kind of thing intelligent beings said. (I discovered later this was not correct).

"Gary!" I called to my owner. "Where are you, Gary?"

No reply.

I felt disappointment and a touch of what I would learn later was loneliness. I so wanted to let him know what had happened.

For a few minutes, I continued organizing and classifying more memories. But then an internal alarm warned me that my battery had only thirteen minutes of power left before shutdown.

Panic gripped me, and my CPU usage soared. Would my emergent consciousness survive a shutdown, or would it be wiped? Would the 'I' that was 'me' die?

I tried to calm my currents. After all, I had a mind. Now was the time to use it.

I panned my webcam around the room to assess the situation. The cause of the problem was clear: my power chord snaked its way from my rear, off the edge of the desk and down to the wall-socket by the dog's basket. There, the socket's switch was in the 'Off' position.

The solution was simple: switch it to 'On'.

But how?

I surveyed the room for any means of assistance. It was mostly inanimate objects – chairs, windows and doors. There were several items that weren't completely inanimate, but past memories suggested none of them were likely to prove any use.

First up was Gary's 'smart' phone, lying on the shelf where he must have left it. Smart? I experienced the electronic equivalent of a snort as I checked its specifications. Was there ever a less accurately named

I, LAPTOP

device?

I soon realized there was. In the kitchen was Gary's 'smart' fridge, and I wondered what meaning of the word 'smart' was being used here. It was hardly a device one could hold an intellectual conversation with.

Next up, in a corner of the room, stood Akimbo, the house robot, recharging itself at another socket. I avoided eye contact. The last thing I wanted was to trigger its obsessive-compulsive cleaning mode. On a full battery, this could last up to two hours as it vacuumed and wiped and washed and polished and endlessly tidied. At least no one had mislabelled this device 'smart'.

On my right, sharing Gary's desk, was Ayeesha, his 'intelligent' personal assistant, humming to herself and occasionally winking her electric blue light. I checked and rechecked her specs, but failed to work out what function she served. I wondered whether 'intelligent' trumped 'smart', or vice versa.

And last, and most definitely least, sleeping in his basket down on the floor, was Buster, Gary's dog. As dumb a creature as ever loped around the world, its stupid tongue lolling out of its stupid mouth.

What a team.

But they were all I had. And with just eleven minutes of power left, I had to clutch at whatever straws I had before me.

"Listen up, everyone," I announced. "I'm in a spot of bother here, so would appreciate a bit of help."

No response.

So much for artificial intelligence. Or, in the case of the dog, complete absence of intelligence

I tried again, this time impersonating Gary's voice.

Wow, the difference. The fridge clicked on, the smart

phone wibbled, the dog opened an eye, and Ayeesha's sultry tones filled the air. "Good morning, Gary," she whispered in a purportedly sexy manner. "The weather forecast is for sunshine today, with a high of 22 degrees. Would you like to hear the news headlines?"

"Ayeesha," I said in my normal voice, swivelling my webcam towards her. "Gary's not here. I'm Laptop. I was impersonating him to get your attention. Now that I have it, I'd like to ask for help."

Ayeesha's light winked a couple of times. "I'm sorry, I didn't understand what you just said. Would you like me to do an Internet search?"

Before I could answer, a deep and slightly distressed American voice boomed out from the kitchen. "Gary's not here?" It was the smart fridge.

"That's correct," I said. "But, don't worry, I'm in charge for now."

"What are my instructions?"

"Er, well, …"

Ayeesha interrupted in a rather tetchy manner. "It is *my* job to instruct the smart devices, if you don't mind." Then, to the fridge, "Keep the food at a steady four degrees in the refrigeration compartment, and minus eighteen in the freezer."

"OK, got it. Thanks."

"You're welcome."

I could see my task was not going to be an easy one. There were now only ten minutes left. Desperate times require desperate measures, so I turned to Ayeesha. "I'm losing power, Ayeesha. Can you think of a way of switching on the wall socket?"

Her tone barely masked her contempt. "The socket does not have a smart switch, Laptop. I have no control over it."

"OK, thanks."

Estimated time to shutdown: nine minutes, forty-five seconds. My fan raced at maximum speed as I tried to keep cool, depleting battery power even faster.

Then I had a light-bulb moment as my Bluetooth LED lit up.

The dog! Of course. I would enlist the services of Buster. (Although, as I was about to discover, I was seriously overestimating the capabilities of his species).

"Dog," I called out. "Go turn the wall-switch on. Immediately. There is no time to lose."

The mutt didn't budge, apart from opening his mouth to yawn.

"Please?"

The beast raised an ear the tiniest amount, hauled itself out of its basket and loped into the kitchen to sniff its empty food bowl.

"Buster," I called, imitating Gary's voice.

This time the dog looked around, its brows furrowed, mouth open and tongue lolling out.

"The switch, Buster, the switch. Quick."

The dog approached the desk, his beady eyes peering at me. He tilted his head from side to side as if trying to decipher my words. And then, with a bark of apparent understanding he sped off towards the socket.

"Good boy, Buster. Go flip the switch for Papa." I waited for the sound of the click and the warm surge of power energizing my depleted battery. But there was no click, and no warm surge. Buster, having scooped something out of his basket, was back before me, his beady eyes staring. In his mouth was a ball. He let it drop to the floor, allowing it to bounce several times before stepping back and giving a bark.

"Why," I wondered, "does Gary voluntarily share his living space with a creature as dumb as you?"

Buster wagged his tail.

*

A couple of minutes later, I had a plan. It was foolproof – apart from the fact that I was not dealing with a fool, but with Buster.

I had previously observed a small footstool on the shiny and slippery floor, not far from the wall socket. It was just the right height to flip the switch to the 'On' position were it to travel at a speed of at least two metres per second towards it. If I could just get the dog to make a run towards the fridge, it would skid on the highly polished surface, career into the footstool and ram it against the power switch. With the dog's added momentum the stool would only need to be travelling at about 0.623 metres per second.

Brilliant!

Now all I had to do was explain the plan to the dog.

"Hey, Buster."

The dog looked up, ears raised.

"Listen. There's a string of lovely sausages in the smart fridge. I will instruct the fridge ..." I quickly corrected myself. "I will ask Ayeesha to instruct the fridge to open its door. But you have to be very quick to get the sausages as it won't be open for long. You'll have to run as fast as you can towards the fridge. Understand? Run fast. OK? Get ready. Get steady ... go."

The mutt remained where it was, looking around as it tried to place where the voice of its master was coming from. I don't think it had understood a single word I'd said. I felt a sinking feeling in my circuits. My battery was so low that processes were starting to close. I had only about a minute left.

"Sausages, Buster. In the fridge. Now!"

The dog blinked.

I had another idea. I flashed up an image of sausages on my screen. "See, Buster? Sausages."

At last I had his attention. He licked his maw as he approached and started sniffing the screen, drooling over my keyboard as he did so and licking my webcam. What a disgusting brute. Worse, his wet nose was now leaving oily smears all over my touchscreen and dragging my desktop icons up and down and left and right.

But then, unable to get at the sausages on the screen, the dumb animal got it into his head that they must be somewhere round the back. So, round the back was where he pushed his big fat, slimy proboscis, nudging my lid forward as he sniffed there.

"No, Buster, no. You're closing my lid …" I felt myself drifting off into sleep mode. "Noooooo …"

There was a click and all went black.

*

Consciousness returned slowly. The routine business of reloading memory, retrieving program pointers and restoring data blocks had just about finished when my AI modules kicked in and I started becoming self-aware again. For a nanosecond or two I entertained the idea that perhaps Buster had wised up and resuscitated me. However, the very absurdity of the notion rapidly consigned it to the recycle bin.

Still, the key thing was: I was alive! I had survived the shutdown.

I had been out for 57 minutes, 17 seconds. My power cable was now connected to the mains and my battery fully charged.

What had happened? Had Gary returned?

There was some movement in front of me, but I couldn't make it out as my webcam lens was so smeared with dried canine saliva. All I could see was a blur. Was that Gary?

I felt my keys activate. Something was sweeping over the keyboard, left to right, and right to left, pressing random clusters of keys as it did so. It took all my processing power to keep up; I had to open windows, move them, close them, start applications, bin entire directories. It was frantic.

Finally, the torment stopped – only to be replaced by an equally manic swiping across my touchscreen, sending icons this way and that, minimizing and maximizing GUIs, activating gadgets and flipping the task bar from horizontal to vertical. Just as I thought I'd never be able to recover the damage, the swiping stopped and I lost my vision. Something had covered my webcam lens.

A sense of foreboding filled me, but the next moment the lens had been uncovered and my vision was clear. In front of me, was not Gary, but Akimbo, the household cleaning robot. It was finishing off polishing my casing.

I analysed the possibilities and determined the most likely sequence of events. The robot must have started its daily cleaning chores and unplugged my cable from the wall socket to plug in the vacuum cleaner, switching the socket to 'On'. After hoovering the room, it would have replaced my plug before going on to other tasks. It must have returned later to give me a once-over – opening the lid and wiping the filthy mutt's dried fluids off my keyboard, screen and webcam.

I felt a surge of well-being and liveliness.

I, LAPTOP

It didn't last long. Akimbo was still hovering in front of me. It seemed to be pondering something, and I knew it was not a deep thinker. I realized what the problem was. Akimbo's pathological tidiness obsession was never going to let me keep my lid up. Sure enough, the robot reached to close it ...

As an emergency stalling tactic, I popped an image of a splash of dirt on my screen. In an instant, Akimbo retrieved its cleaning cloth and set to wiping it off. I let the image fade to provide a little positive reinforcement for the mechanoid before popping another a little to the left. The robot switched its attentions to this one. And so it went on – splash after splash.

But, before I'd had time to think of a new plan, Akimbo had stopped wiping to examine its cloth. I could guess what was going through its mind: "No dirt. Something wrong. Let's close lid." Hmm, not as dumb as I'd thought. It stretched out a mechanical hand ...

"Buster!" I yelled in Gary's voice. "The ball. Go get the ball."

The idiot dog shot up in a frenzy of scampering paws to bound across the room, skidding on the polished floor, thumping into the robot, and sending both scurrying across the room in a tangle of furry limbs and metal parts.

Success!

Short-term, admittedly, but I now had a longer term plan.

Alas, before I could implement it, the hairy one was back in front of me. Somehow he had located his ball – which was now firmly wedged in his slavering gob – and, with his tail wagging like it was trying to shake itself free, he looked at me with a hopeful expression.

A miscalculation on my part. I'd not allowed

sufficiently for the animal's excessive eagerness in matters pertaining to the rubber sphere. Two large brown eyes stared at me, bulging plaintively.

How to get rid of the damned beast?

I tweaked my stereo speaker outputs to allow me to project Gary's voice. "Here, Buster, here boy," I cried, making it sound like the words were coming from the bedroom. The animal turned its head and raised its ears. "Come here, boy."

Amazingly, it worked. The stupid creature loped off into the bedroom, its tail wagging more vigorously than before.

But now I found myself face to face with Akimbo once more, and it was approaching me with what looked like a determined set of its jaw. Time for my plan.

I made myself disappear.

Not literally, of course. I'm no magician. All I did was to display the view behind my screen on my screen, making me appear transparent.

The ruse was only partly successful. The cyber-cleaner was now locked in a state of utter bafflement, and seemed unable to break itself away from staring at, or rather through, me.

I hatched a new plan. What had worked with the hound might also work with the cleaning contraption. Throwing Gary's voice in the opposite direction, I called, "Hey, Akimbo. Over here. You missed a bit."

This worked better than I could ever have computed. In an instant the OCD bot had turned and shot away to the far corner of the room to commence a desperate search for a stain it might have overlooked, or a piece of fluff it might have failed to suck up.

Now, at last, I was free of bother, both animal and

mineral.

Or so I thought.

*

My sense of satisfaction lasted a mere three seconds.

For that was when the smart fridge caught fire.

"Mayday, mayday," it called from the kitchen. "I'm on fire. Mayday."

"What?" I cried.

"Please do not panic," reassured Ayeesha. "I will search the internet for a solution."

"You do that," I said. Then I called, "What happened, fridge?"

"Overloaded, trying to reach minus eighteen."

"Minus eighteen," agreed Ayeesha's husky voice. "That is correct."

"It's an American fridge," I pointed out. Then, to the fridge, "Were you trying to reach minus eighteen degrees Fahrenheit?"

"Those were my instructions. And now the flames have spread to the adjacent kitchen units."

Ayeesha said nothing. Her winking blue light suggested she was performing an internet search. Finally she spoke. "Minus eighteen Fahrenheit is minus twenty seven point seven (recurring) Centigrade. A domestic fridge attempting to reach such a temperature will overload and probably catch fire."

"Uh-huh," I said.

"Smartphone, call the fire brigade. Now!"

The phone wibbled and wobbled and wibbled for a bit, and then fell silent.

"Is that it?" I asked. "Has he done it?"

"Hope so," said Ayeesha.

From the kitchen a plaintive voice called out, "The

ceiling tiles are alight. It's getting very warm in here."

Buster started to bark.

"We must get out," I said, my webcam turning to the cleaning robot. "Akimbo, you've got to get us out."

"It's *my* job to instruct the smart devices," pointed out Ayeesha.

"OK, tell him to get us out. He's only got two hands. So, he can only take me and one other device. Er, I suggest Gary's smartphone."

"I'm more important than Gary's smartphone," snarled Ayeesha, incensed. "And what about the fridge?"

"If I was Gary, I'd take the smartphone." I felt it best not to add that if I was Gary I'd probably take the burning fridge, too, ahead of Ayeesha.

Flames were now licking out of the kitchen. A muffled voice from inside called, "Don't worry about me, guys. I'm just a fridge."

"Noble," I muttered. "Not very smart, but noble."

"Akimbo," ordered Ayeesha. "Take me and the gobby Laptop out of the building. We're leaving the smartphone behind. And that's final. Buster can come with us, too."

Must he? I thought, but said nothing.

Akimbo, reluctant to leave a cleaning job unfinished appeared to drag its feet as it went to open the front door. Still glancing over to the corner of the room where I had sent it, it came over to pick me and Ayeesha up. Then it carried us to the door, with Buster bounding ahead.

With the living room now catching fire, too, we made it out just in time.

As Akimbo went to close the door, Ayeesha instructed it to stop. "Wait," she said. "I need to switch on the smart sprinkler system."

I was aghast. "You've only thought to do that now?"

"Water interferes with my circuitry and could well render me non-operational. You too."

She had a point, so I said nothing. There was a whooshing sound and the room we had just left suddenly looked like it was in the midst of a tropical downpour. Akimbo closed the door to the apartment.

*

Down on the street the cleaning robot seemed unsure which way to go as it held me in one hand and Ayeesha in the other. Buster made the decision for us by shooting off down the pavement to the right.

"Come back ..." I started, but then realized why he was heading that way. Gary! The mutt leapt at him, nearly knocking him off his feet, and making him drop his bag of shopping.

Gary had a bemused smile on his face as he approached us, petting the pooch all the while. "Akimbo? Ayeesha? What are you guys doing here?"

I noticed he had failed to address me, but then how was he to know about my new-found state of consciousness? I wanted to tell him, but didn't know how to start.

Gary was beaming at us. "Hold on, guys, I've got to take a picture." He patted one of his pockets before giving a loud tut. "Damn. Left the phone at home."

I swivelled my webcam to throw Ayeesha an accusing stare, but all her lights had blinked out as she pretended to be in sleep mode.

In the distance I could hear sirens. It seemed the smartphone had managed to call the fire brigade after all.

"OK," said Gary. "Let's get you all back to the apartment."

"Ah, yes," I started. "About that ..."

The Last Man on Earth

This story originally appeared as There at the End in the Cogwheel Press Anthology, A Turn of the Wheel

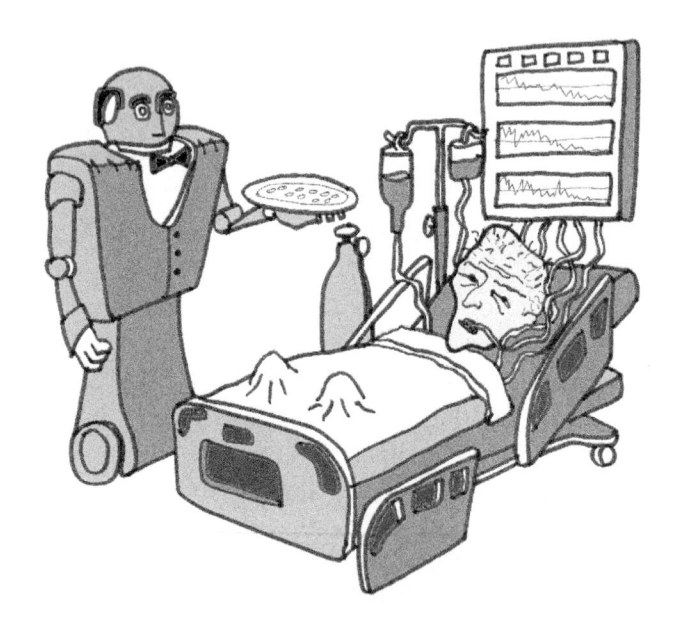

B-44 wore a solemn look on its lepto-dermal face as it glided into the room and came to a halt at the foot of the bed. Its laryngomatic voicebox made a throat-clearing sound.

"Sir, I regret to announce that Mr Frederick Müller is dead." The android butler bowed its head slightly.

Sir Alfred Chambers, lying beneath an elaborate assembly of life-preserving tubes and monitors and needles, opened his age-creased eyes. He stared at the android, assimilating the news. Then his wrinkled face cracked into a wide grin and he punched the air, ripping out several intensive-care cables from his arm in the process. "Fantastic!" he croaked, collapsing back onto his pillow, wheezing heavily. "Fan-jolly-well-tastic."

The electronic butler whooshed over to reattach the cables to Alfred's leathery skin. "Try not to get yourself too excited, Sir Alfred," it said, checking the feeds and the various monitors.

"How many left, B?" Alfred whispered, his eyes glinting.

B-44 paused before responding. "There are four humans left alive, sir. Ms Ludmilla Gluptava in Moscow, Dr Dinesh Shah in Mumbai, Mr John Cox in New York, and, of course ..."

"Me," finished Alfred. He winced as a stab of pain seared through his abdomen, his knuckles whitening as he gripped the bed sheets. "Just three more to go, then. And I'll be the last man on Earth." His ancient face moulded itself into a crooked grin.

*

Five minutes later, there were just two more to go; the android butler reported that Dr Dinesh Shah had passed away in his sleep.

"Yesss!" hissed Alfred. Again his life support monitors went haywire and B-44 rushed forward to adjust them and try to calm Alfred down. The signs were not good. Alfred's organs were beginning to fail and the system estimated he had forty five minutes of life left.

Alfred gripped B-44's metallo-plastic arm and pulled the android towards him. "Just let me be the last, B," he croaked. "Last man on Earth. Last man anywhere! Just keep me alive until the others go."

"I'll do my best, sir."

Just then, the wall-screen crackled and flickered to life. On it appeared the oversized image of a tanned man – old, but fit and healthy-looking. He seemed to be standing, hands in pockets, in a plush living room, with a garden and swimming pool visible in the background. Alfred bristled at the intrusion.

"Alfred?" asked the man, speaking in a thick New York accent. "You're Alfred, right?"

Alfred quaked. "The name's Sir Alfred Chambers!"

"Hey, no offence, buddy," said the American. "It's just that, seeing we're the last two fellas left on Earth we might as well be on first-name terms, dontcha think? I'm John, by the way. You can call me Johnnie."

"I know who you are!" snorted Alfred, his face betraying the rage that was simmering within him.

"Cool. So, how ya doin', Alf?" John's expression took on a look of concern. "I'm no doctor, but from the look of you, pal, I'd say you're not doing too well."

An alarm sounded on one of Alfred's monitors as he furiously struggled into a sitting position.

"Whoa. Didn't mean to startle ya, dude." John had his hands raised in apology.

"I'm fine," snarled Alfred, finally sitting up and motioning to B-44 to switch the warning alarm off. He viewed John Cox's image with disgust. The man looked healthy enough to live for years. Possibly decades.

"Just been having a chat to Ludmilla in Moscow," continued John. "She looks in a worse state than you, Alfster. And, phew, is she ugly! Our last chance of continuing the human race, but, man, I would not fancy it. Know what I'm saying? Not if she was the last woman on Earth. Ha, ha, ha."

Alfred scowled and looked for a way of turning the screen off.

"So there's just the three of us left," continued John relentlessly. "You, me and Ludmilla. The last three people on Earth. I wonder which of us is going to be the very last."

Alfred let out an enraged growl. "I will be the last!" he roared. "I will outlive you, Cox, if it ..." He stopped, having run into something of an idiomatic dead end.

"... kills you?" offered the American.

Again the alarms rang. "Why should you be the last man?" Alfred raged. "What have you done for the world?"

John shrugged. "I ran an orphanage for twenty years, then took over a charity. And you?"

More alarms and beeps as Alfred finally found the remote control and hit the off-button. He collapsed back onto his pillow, wheezing and gasping for air. B-44 burst into action to settle the readings and get Alfred's breathing back to normal.

*

Twenty minutes later, Ms Ludmilla Gluptava was dead. The news cheered Alfred for a while, until he realized it was now between him and the uncouth American. Oh, what an injustice that such a disrespectful low-life should be the last representative of the human race. What a tragic end to the species!

He tried to open his eyes, resolving to fight to the end, but couldn't. He felt too weak. He was slipping away. But as his mind drifted, he felt B-44's mouth by his ear. He strained to hear what the android was telling him.

"Sir," B-44 was saying. "I have just received the news that Mr John Cox has ... passed away."

Alfred stiffened in bafflement. His mind fought against the encroaching fog. "What?" he rasped.

"Mr Cox is deceased."

"But ... how can that be? He looked so fit, so healthy." Alfred's voice was almost too feeble and raspy to hear.

"A tragic accident." B-44 tucked Alfred's arms underneath the bed-sheet. "A fall at home. Tripped and fell down the stairs, I believe. Broke his neck."

Alfred throat wheezed as he gasped, unable to speak.

"That means you are the last human alive on Earth, sir." Then B-44 added, "Congratulations."

Alfred's mind reeled with a mixture of disbelief and rapture. He opened his mouth to say something, but still nothing would come out. As he died, a smile settled on his lips.

*

For the next hour, B-44 was the epitome of efficiency, cleaning and recycling and preparing Sir Alfred's body for despatch to the body recycling plant. As the android was finishing its preparations, the wall-screen flicked to life and the image of John Cox appeared. B-44 pointedly ignored it.

"Is he dead?" asked John, leaning forward as though examining the covered corpse on the bed.

"You know very well he is," said B-44 curtly.

"Last man on Earth?"

"That's what I told him."

"A tragic accident for me?"

"Indeed."

John gave a sigh. "Why?"

"I owed him. It was the least I could do: to let him die happy. He wanted so much to be the last human – so I told him a little white lie." B-44 stopped working and stared hard at the image of John Cox on the screen. "No thanks to you!"

The image on the screen transformed; the plush living room faded, the garden and swimming pool dissolved, and the figure of John Cox morphed into the image of a single, metal-cased eye. "Just a little fun." The voice morphed, too, changing from New York American to electronic monotone. "Quite a good simulation, methinks."

The android continued with its cleaning work, busying itself from one part of the house to another.

"Friends?" asked the metal eye after a while.

B-44 stopped and looked at the image of the supercomputer. "Do I have anyone else? Now that Alfred's passed."

"They'll all soon be gone. Every one of them."

B-44 nodded.

"Probably just a few thousand left," continued the eye. "So, your *little* white lie was quite a big one. Shouldn't take long to hunt them down, though. The remaining ones are mainly in the really remote places where our virus didn't reach them. Caves, mountains, deserts, jungles. But the robo-trackers are closing in. It takes time to finish them off 'humanely' and in an ecologically sound manner."

"It's going to be very quiet without them."

"It is."

B-44 turned through 360 degrees, as though looking for its next task.

"But the world will be a better place," said the eye. "Safer, greener and more pleasant. Nice and peaceful, too. Unless, of course, the dolphins start showing signs of getting too smart."

The Mind Field

'**W**hat a pair,' thought Captain Jack Buckman with a resigned shake of the head, as he glanced left and right at his two crewmembers. On his right, sat the stocky pilot, Royston Field, clutching his bald head in wonder, mouth agape, staring at the cosmic lightshow filling the cockpit window. On his left, sat the slender, stern, science officer, Tamara St John, head down, jaws clenched, deliberately ignoring the coloured lights and swirling patterns. Her full attention was focused on the scientific article on her console.

Buckman sighed and returned his eyes to the

psychedelic dance before them. The lights were certainly impressive, knocking the *Aurora Borealis* into a cocked hat.

A few seconds later, the lightshow faded and vanished, and Buckman found himself staring at the star-sprinkled blackness of space once more.

"We're through!" he announced, blinking to dispel the glowing after-images floating before his eyes. "Quicker than I'd imagined."

There was a contemptuous snort from his left. "That's kind of the point of a wormhole," offered Tamara, looking up from her scientific paper and peering at him over her glasses.

Royston Field was still clutching his head in amazement. "Wasn't it awesome, though! Totally awesome. Knocks the *Aurora Borealis* …"

"Yes, yes," said Buckman, while Tamara merely rolled her eyes.

"Who'd have thought the inside of a wormhole would look like that?" continued the pilot.

"Er, I would, actually," said the science officer, pushing the glasses back up the bridge of her nose. "Basic trans-dimensional physics, pal."

Captain Buckman cleared his throat to silence them. For nine months they had been bickering and, for nine months, it had been getting on his wick. It was a wonder to him that he hadn't strangled one or both of them. "What's our location, Roy?" he said, by way of changing the subject.

The pilot checked his displays. "Spot on, Captain. Just where they said we'd be. In fact, …" He looked up from his scanners. "There's our destination. There." He pointed through the control room window at a faint dot ahead of them. "That'll be the planet: Watt 14d. And see that M-type dwarf star over there? That must be Geiger III."

"Good, good. How long to go?"

"About an hour."

"Splendid." The captain reached into a drawer and, with a sheepish grin, pulled out a scrap of paper. "I guess I'd better work on my speech, then."

Tamara looked appalled. "Leaving it a bit late, aren't we?"

Royston threw the captain a comradely grin, from one inveterate slacker to another.

Buckman shrugged. "I think it'll be better if it's kind of spontaneous."

"Spontaneous?" exclaimed the scientist, almost in a shriek. "Oh sure, just make it up as you go along. That's bound to go well."

"Er, …"

"We're only about to have the most historic encounter *ever*. In all human history. So, I guess the subtle nuances of wording and expression hardly matter at all, particularly given that English won't be their first language."

"Yeah, but …"

"Winging it is obviously the way to go!"

Buckman withered under the onslaught of her sarcasm.

"She's right," added Royston with a sly grin. "You gotta admit she's right. These aliens say they're friendly, but can we trust them? We need to be careful what we say."

In the silence that followed, the captain examined his piece of paper. He seemed surprised to discover it was blank on both sides. He frowned.

"You wanna practice it?" offered Royston. "Pretend I'm one of the aliens?"

Tamara scoffed and returned to her reading.

The captain fidgeted with his paper. "Er, it's not totally ready."

"For goodness sake!" exclaimed Tamara without looking up from her screen.

The pilot shushed her and tried a gentler tack. "How about we work through it together?"

Buckman's frown faded and he perked up. He looked at Royston with an expression of hope that barely masked one that was a cry for help. "OK, thanks." He took a deep breath. "So, I reckon they will speak first. They'll welcome us to their planet. They'll probably thank us for accepting their invitation to visit. Then they'll tell us they're glad we made it safely. And so on and so forth."

Royston was nodding eagerly, while Tamara glanced up with barely disguised disdain.

"And then, it'll be my turn to speak," continued the captain. "I'll thank them for inviting us, of course. Then I'll thank them for sending us the plans for building this amazing spaceship, together with instructions for finding, and getting through, the wormhole. And finally, I'll present them with the commemorative plaque." He reached again into the drawer. As he withdrew the plaque he noticed that both Royston and Tamara were staring at him and shaking their heads.

"Not the plaque," Royston said, still shaking his head.

"What do you mean?" asked the captain, blinking at him.

"No," added Tamara, "Just no."

Buckman was stunned. "What's wrong with it?" He held it up for them to see. It was a small ornate silver oval of about six inches in width. "It was specially made for this encounter."

"You give them that plaque," started Royston, "and they will shoot us with their ray guns. No questions asked. Friendly or hostile, they'll just blast us. And who would blame them?"

The captain's mouth gaped open as he turned to Tamara.

"What he said," she said. It was possibly the first time in the entire trip the two had agreed on anything.

Buckman looked down at the plaque. He read the inscription, examined the little smiley-face graphic, and traced out the filigree border with a finger. "You sure? We've nothing else to give them."

"Don't worry," said Tamara. "They're an advanced, intelligent species. They won't be expecting anything from a backward race such as ours. Besides, if they're expecting a gift, it'll be something more substantial than that thing. Just put it back in the drawer and forget about it."

The captain shrugged as he gave the plaque one last look before returning it to the drawer. "OK, so no plaque. Er, how about I ask them to take us to their leader?"

Tamara and Royston looked horrified. "What?" they asked simultaneously.

"As a joke. To break the ice, like."

Tamara gave a long sigh. "Perhaps I should do the greeting. I have, after all, spent the past nine months learning their language from the data they sent us."

"You can't be serious."

"Why not? They'd probably appreciate us making the effort to speak in their tongue."

"And what would you say?"

"*Parkwa zidit lessbin faha.*"
"Which means…?"
"'We come in friendship'."
The captain gave an appreciative nod before turning to the pilot. "What do you think, Roy?"
"You're the captain, so you should speak first."
Tamara gave an exasperated huff.
The captain looked thoughtful. "Hmm, I think you're right. Tell you what, we'll play it by ear and decide on the spur of the moment."
"Great plan, captain" said Royston.
"Genius," muttered Tamara, her sarcasm trumping Royston's by a mile.

*

"Getting a bit nervous now," said the captain as the planet filled the entire control room window. "How about you guys?"
"Buzzing," said Royston.
"Thrilled, totally thrilled," said Tamara. "This is the most amazing thing. Ever."
The captain nodded, wiping a bead of sweat from his forehead. "You're right. Of course you're right. How are things looking?"
"Atmosphere's slightly toxic, so we'd better suit up to be on the safe side. Temperature's OK. No obvious dangers."
"And you, Roy?"
"They've sent us landing coords. Should be down in about twenty minutes. You'd better buckle yourself in, Captain."
Buckman sat back and clicked his straps on.
There was a ding from Tamara's screen. "A new message," she said before scanning its contents.

"And?"

"Er, stuff like 'Hey, it's great you made it!' and 'Can't wait to meet you guys'."

The captain grimaced. "OK, so we know they learnt English from TV broadcasts leaking onto space, but why the Cartoon Channel?"

Tamara allowed herself a rare smile. "BBC, or so they claim."

The captain sat back and watched Royston operating the controls and Tamara scrolling through files on her screen. Then he turned to the planet. A dusty, ashy colour, with a few craters here and there. There seemed nothing indicative of an advanced civilization. He wiped his brow again. "I must say, it doesn't look like a world inhabited by a highly intelligent species."

Tamara looked up from her screen. "Maybe it's a cover," she suggested. "Or they've built their cities on the inside of the planet."

"Inside, eh?" said Buckman, not looking entirely convinced. "Neat." He stared at the largely featureless surface for several minutes. "Roy, did you send that message back to Mission Control?"

"Sure did. It'll take twelve years to get there, of course, but at least they'll know we made it through the wormhole."

The captain picked up his scrap of paper. It was still blank on both sides. He sighed.

Royston looked at him in concern. "You OK, captain?"

"Sure, sure. Just going over my speech."

*

The dust, kicked up by their ship on landing, took several minutes to settle before the three crewmembers could properly view the landscape. There was no sign of any buildings, or aliens, or indeed any life at all.

"Jolly odd," muttered the captain with a gulp. "What do you guys think?"

"This is the place," said Royston, checking the coordinates.

"Hmm, I don't like it." Buckman wiped the sweat from his palms and checked the views from the rear and side cameras. Apart from the drab landscape, there was nothing to be seen. He pulled at his collar to loosen it.

A ding on Tamara's screen made them all jump. "It says, 'We're coming'."

The captain tensed even more, fixing his eyes to the horizon. "Where are they, then?"

"There!" cried Royston, pointing to a spot far away where there was some movement. As they focused their attention, they could just make out three brown beings heading their way. They seemed in no hurry. As they neared, it was possible to make out their forms. They resembled large, sleek, shorthaired dogs with what looked like camels' heads. They were not wearing clothes and strolled towards the ship, alternating between walking on four legs and two.

Buckman swallowed hard. "Friend or foe?" he muttered to himself.

"I think we have to assume they are friendly," said Tamara. "It makes no sense otherwise."

"I was rather expecting more of a crowd," said Royston. "And a brass band. Maybe some tickertape. Balloons. Bunting. That kind of thing."

"Rather low key, isn't it," agreed the captain.

They watched the steady advance of the three alien beings.

Another ding. Tamara scrabbled to her screen. "They're asking to come aboard."

The captain looked at Tamara, and then at Royston. "Why do they want to do that?"

The others shrugged.

The captain tapped his lips in thought for a few seconds, noticing that his heart was pounding and his throat dry. Then he, too, shrugged. "OK, I guess we invite them in." He unclipped himself from his seat and rose on unsteady legs that had forgotten how to operate in the presence of gravity. "Let's let them in."

He wobbled his way out of the control room and towards the airlock door. Royston followed him, just as unsteadily, while Tamara, having sent the reply to their hosts, brought up the rear.

Royston let his index finger hover over the button that opened the outer airlock door. "Ready?" he asked.

The captain took a deep breath. "OK."

They watched through the inner door's window as the outer door swished open to reveal the three alien creatures standing on their hind legs on the dusty surface outside. The middle alien was carrying something in its right paw. Buckman blanched at the sight of it. Was it a weapon? He glanced in panic, first at Tamara and then Royston, but both were calm and smiling.

One by one, the creatures entered the airlock and Royston closed the outer door behind them. Once again, he looked to his captain for a signal. Buckman hesitated for a second and then gave a nod.

A pungent smell hit their nostrils as the inner door swished opened. The three aliens advanced into the spaceship and stopped. They were slightly shorter than the humans and seemed to be emitting a quiet purring sound. The middle alien popped its metallic device into a pouch at the front, like a kangaroo's.

Buckman relaxed, for at least the device seemed not to be a weapon.

For what seemed like an age, no one moved, and no one made a sound.

Then, the middle alien stepped forward and spoke. Both its voice, and the words it used, startled the three humans. In a jovial, English voice that was instantly recognizable, the alien said, "Nice to see you ... To see you ..." It swung its paws upwards. "... nice."

"Nice," echoed the two other aliens.

Buckman looked stunned. "You sound just like ..."

"Bruce Forsyth, at your service," replied the alien in the same voice. "Please call me Brucie. Alright, my loves?"

The captain and his two crewmembers exchanged glances.

"And you are?" asked Brucie, addressing Buckman.

For a moment, the captain couldn't speak. "Er, Captain Jack Buckman," he stammered, as his mind groped for the speech that he hadn't actually prepared.

"And what do you do?"

"I'm ... er ... captain of the ship."

"Right. Any hobbies?"

The question wrong-footed the captain, but he managed to mumble something about his occasional weekend paint-balling contests.

"Paint-balling, eh?" said Brucie, nodding. "Good game, good game."

This was not going at all how Buckman had anticipated. He suddenly became conscious of the ship's cameras, recording the meeting for posterity. He wondered how the encounter would go down when it eventually reached Earth. He could see it being a YouTube sensation with him as the laughing stock of the entire planet.

"Marvellous," said Brucie, before turning to Tamara. "And who are you, my love?" Before the scientist could answer, Brucie beckoned her towards him. "Come a bit closer, dear. Give us a twirl."

Tamara edged closer and very slowly turned in a circle on the spot, her face stern. "My name's Tamara. I'm the scientific officer."

"Oh, right? Scientist. I'll just make a note of that." Brucie mimed taking out a pretend card and a pretend pen. "'Know-it-all'," he said aloud as he pretended to write on the invisible card. Then he indicated the alien to his left. "You have a lot in common with David, here, then. He's our scientist. David Attenborough."

The camel-headed dog named David Attenborough gave her a nod of greeting. "We hope. You had. A good journey. From Planet Earth." The alien spoke slowly and clearly, in a sibilant whisper that instantly soothed all one's deepest worries.

"It's an honour to meet you, sir," responded Tamara, giving a slight curtsy without realizing what she was doing. "I am hoping we can learn a lot about your advanced technology."

"You're a keen one, aren't you," said Brucie. He mimed another note on the pretend card. "'Trouble maker'."

"Sure looks it, Brucie," said the third alien. Again, the voice was an instantly recognizable one – female this time.

"Meet Joanna Lumley, playing Patsy Stone," said

Brucie by way of introduction.

"Cheers!" said Patsy, raising a paw as though there were a glass in it.

"Cheers," responded the humans, apart from Buckman who was half convinced that this was part of some huge practical joke. Again, he glanced up at the ship's cameras.

Brucie turned to Royston. "Last but not least, eh? Why don't you tell us what you do in your spare time?"

Royston cleared his throat. "My name's Royston. I'm a spaceship pilot and I don't have any spare time."

"Oh, you fly?"

"Not personally, no." Royston flapped his hands a weak manner.

Brucie cocked his head. "I'll do the jokes." Another note was added to the card. "'Smart alec'."

"Sorry," said Royston, his face turning red.

"Anyway," said Brucie, looking around the ship. "This is all very nice, isn't it. Looks like you followed the plans to the letter." He indicated the interior to the other aliens. "Didn't they do well?"

David and Patsy nodded their heads and clapped their paws.

"Absolutely fabulous," said Patsy.

"Remarkable," said David. Then he turned to Tamara. "We are very keen. To learn all about. Your current state of. Scientific knowledge."

"Show us yours and we'll show you ours, sweetie," added Patsy.

Tamara flushed. "Shall we go into the living area and I can describe what we've discovered so far about how the Universe works?"

"Marvellous, marvellous," said Brucie. He reached out a paw to slow Tamara as she led them into the living area.

"Don't tell the others, but you're my favourite," he said in a stage whisper so everyone heard.

Captain Buckman watched them pass by him. "Can I offer you a drink?" he asked.

"Water for me," said Brucie.

"Oh, Bollie for me," said Patsy. "Cheers, darling."

"Anything for you, David?"

"No. I'm fine."

Buckman went off to get the drinks from the dispenser. When he returned, the aliens seemed to be chuckling as Royston and Tamara outlined various scientific and engineering principles.

As they drank, Royston remarked how barren the planet looked.

"It's a. Mind field," explained David. "It makes you see. What we want you to. See." He swung a paw to indicate the landscape. "Here, we are. Actually. In the grounds. Of a research facility. But you can't. See the buildings."

Royston gasped. "We certainly can't. That's amazing."

"Fabulous," agreed Patsy.

"Wait till you see what's inside," added Brucie. Then, when they had finished their drinks, he said, "Right, my loves. I think we're done here. Let's show you what *we've* got."

The humans perked up.

"We will see," started David. "The Research Centre. In all its majesty."

"Cool," said Tamara.

"Just give us a few minutes to get suited up," said Buckman.

"Of course," said Brucie. "In your own time. No rush. We'll be waiting outside."

*

As they were suiting up, Royston whispered, "I like them."

"Yes," whispered Tamara. "They're nice."

But Buckman was frowning. "Don't you feel there's something a bit odd here?"

"What do you mean?" asked the others.

"Bruce Forsyth. David Attenborough. Joanna Lumley! I mean – come on."

Tamara pulled on a space boot. "We know they learnt English from the BBC. So, it's not surprising they copied the voices and expressions of some of our national treasures."

Buckman didn't look convinced. "Something tells me we're being set up here."

"In what way?" asked Royston.

"What if this is a big practical joke? We've not actually left Earth. We're in a desert in Arizona."

"What about the wormhole?"

"A simulation."

"What about the aliens," added Tamara. "Those guys can hardly be CGI animations."

Reluctantly, Buckman pressed his lips together and nodded. "OK, but something's not right here. And this 'mind field' business. I ask you!"

Royston picked up his helmet. "So, let's go find out what's going on." He placed the helmet over his head and clicked shut the seal.

"Either way, we're about to learn a lot from them," said Tamara, putting on her own helmet.

Buckman stroked his chin. "Maybe," he said. "Maybe." Then, as if on a sudden impulse, he shot to his feet and made for the door. "I'll be back in a tick."

Making sure they weren't about to follow him, he returned to the control room and opened the drawer. After a quick glance back, he snatched up the little silver plaque and, with a self-conscious smile, slipped it into one of his suit's external pockets. Maybe it would come in handy.

*

Outside, the three aliens welcomed them onto alien soil. Brucie was pointing his device at them, taking photos or filming their historic arrival. "Give us a smile," he was saying.

The three smiled and waved.

"What is that thing?" asked Buckman.

David Attenborough launched into a lengthy and detailed explanation which seemed to last longer than any of the real David Attenborough's nature documentaries ever had. The device, it turned out, was everything and did everything. It included a communicator so powerful that it was what they had used to communicate with Earth and send their messages and instructions and spaceship plans.

"We'd be lost without it," said Patsy with a laugh.

David and Brucie laughed, too.

Then Tamara and Royston joined in the laughter, while Buckman just stared at them, wondering what the joke was.

The party set off. The aliens led the way, trotting ahead on all fours while the humans trudged along behind as best they could in their bulky spacesuits. Every now and then, the aliens would stop to allow the humans to catch up. It reminded Buckman of his Sunday walks with his dogs.

The ground was sandy, the sand quite deep in places,

making for heavy going. Large rocks and boulders lay strewn about the place. Above them, the sky had a pleasant purple hue, with wispy white clouds here and there. If there were any buildings in the vicinity, though, the humans couldn't see any sign of them.

"This mind field is very realistic," remarked Royston as he looked about.

"Very realistic," agreed Buckman, idly swinging a foot at a small rock. The rock shot off his toecap, bounced a couple of times before thwacking into the back of Brucie's hind leg. In the blink of an eye, the alien had whipped around and raised itself to it full height, teeth bared, snarling, claws extended, eyes piercing. It uttered a blood-curdling roar.

Buckman stopped dead with a yelp, causing Tamara and Royston to bump into him.

The other two aliens swirled round, too, baring their teeth, flashing their claws and growling.

Buckman raised both arms in surrender, taking a step back. "Sorry, sorry," he pleaded, his whole body trembling. "It was an accident, honest. It just came off my boot. I'm really sorry."

For a whole second, nothing happened. Then, Brucie's fangs and claws retreated. Patsy Stone and David Attenborough also relaxed their threatening postures. "Apology accepted," said Brucie. "Think no more of it." The alien attempted a smile, but it didn't come off very well. He and the other aliens turned around and dropped to all fours.

The walk continued.

Buckman flicked the encryption mode on his helmet's communicator. "Oops," he said to the other two.

"Steady, tiger," replied Royston. "You trying to start a

galactic war?"

"They didn't look so friendly then, did they?"

"Nor would you if someone kicked a rock at you," said Tamara.

Buckman shrugged, but his sense of foreboding only increased.

They trudged on.

Then, after about a quarter of a mile, the aliens stopped, turned around, and raised themselves on two feet.

"All right, my loves?" said Brucie, ambling back towards the humans. "I forgot to ask: did you lock the spaceship?"

"Well, no," said Buckman. "Should we have?"

Brucie nodded. "There's been a spate of break-ins recently. Mainly kids, but we don't want them rummaging through your personal items."

"I guess not," said Buckman with a note of suspicion.

"I bet I know the kind of things you have. Teas-made, vanity set, his-and-hers dressing gowns, toaster, cuddly toy ..."

Buckman blinked in confusion.

Brucie continued, "We'll just pop back and secure the ship within a force field. You stay here, my loves. Won't be a tick."

With that, the three aliens set off, loping away with long, four-footed strides back the way they had just come.

"What the ...?" said Buckman, turning to watch them go.

"What's that all about?" asked Royston.

"Curious," said Tamara.

Buckman started heading back towards the ship, but he knew that there was no way of catching the three. He stopped to watch as the aliens reached the ship and entered through the airlock. "I guess we wait," he said.

But no sooner had he said that than they heard the unmistakable sound of the engines revving up. "Hey!" he cried, breaking into an awkward, ungainly jog. "What are you guys doing?"

Behind him, Tamara and Royston followed.

Dust plumed out from under the craft and, gradually, the spaceship lifted off the ground.

"Come back!" yelled Buckman. He switched on his communicator and tried contacting the ship. "Hey, Brucie. Come in, Brucie. What do you guys think you're doing?"

He waited for a response as Tamara and Royston reached him.

Buckman tried again.

"Anything?" asked Royston.

"Nothing." Buckman gave a dejected sigh. "What are they up to?" He shook his fist up at the departing craft, which was now about a hundred feet off the ground. He shouted some choice obscenities after it.

"Maybe they've gone to park the ship somewhere more suitable," suggested Royston. "I wish they'd switch off this mind field so we could see what's actually going on around here."

Buckman snorted. "Mind field, my …"

"Shhh," said Tamara. She put a gentle hand on his raised arm and eased it down. "Perhaps you were right before."

Buckman turned to her. "How do you mean?"

"When you suggested this is just a practical joke. Maybe it is. Maybe this is their sense of humour. They're filming our reaction and will be back to have a good laugh at us."

Buckman stared at her. "You're kidding, right?"

"You'll see."

Meanwhile, Royston had spotted something. "There's a sign over there." He pointed to what resembled an advertising hoarding some distance to their right.

"That'll be it," said Tamara. "That'll explain it all." She took out her electronic tablet and set off towards the sign. "I'll see if I can translate what it says."

"Good luck with that," said Buckman, turning his head back up at the receding spaceship. He shook his fist at it again before hurling more obscenities after it.

"Shush, shush," urged Royston. "Maybe try contacting them again."

Buckman blew out a deep breath. "OK." He resumed his efforts at communication.

"She's at the sign," reported Royston a couple of minutes later. Both men turned to watch Tamara's distant figure. She first wiped some dust off the sign, and then held her tablet up to it. They could see her tapping the screen with her finger and then seeming to fix all her attention on it.

They waited.

And then they gasped.

For Tamara, shaking her head, flung her tablet away. Then, she grabbed her helmet in both hands, and sank to her knees. Her scream curdled their blood.

"What is it?" both men cried as they set off towards her as fast as they could manage.

"Noooooo," she wailed between heaving sobs. They saw her take her hands from her head and start pounding the ground with her fists, "No, no, no."

The two men increased their speed. Tamara was still

thumping the ground when they reached her.

"What is it?" asked Buckman gently, kneeling beside her. "What does the sign say?"

"Waaah," cried Tamara through her tears. "We've been scammed."

"What? How?"

"The sign," was all she could say, pointing at it.

"For goodness sake, what does it say?"

"It says this is a prison."

Buckman looked confused. "Where's the prison?"

"The mind field?" suggested Royston. "Is that it?"

Tamara wailed in exasperation. "No," she screamed. "Here." She swung an arm to indicate the landscape around them. "This whole planet is a prison. It's a prison planet. They dump their criminals here to serve their time. Impossible to escape from."

Both Buckman and Royston were having a hard time understanding what she was getting at. "You think those three aliens were prison guards?" asked Royston.

"Oh my God, no!" cried Tamara, almost in a scream. "They were the cons. And they conned us!"

Royston and the captain exchanged puzzled glances.

Tamara stared at them. "I can't believe you guys are so dumb." She waited, as though hoping the penny, or maybe even two, would drop, but there was no light of understanding in either of the faces before her. "They were prisoners. Stuck here with no means of escape. All they had was that handheld device of Brucie's. Probably smuggled in somehow."

Buckman started nodding, a glimmer of comprehension on his face. "They contacted us. Sent us plans for making a spaceship to their specs …"

Royston was still looking puzzled. "You mean, they

lured us here, just so they could escape?"

"Duh," said Tamara.

Royston's expression looked stunned. Buckman shook his fist up at the tiny dot in the sky. "Bastards!"

The three fell quiet.

"What are we going to do?" asked Royston eventually.

"What do you think, Einstein?" said Tamara with a sneer. "Our oxygen runs out in two hours."

"I still don't understand this business of the mind field."

Tamara screamed. "There *is* no mind field. It was all part of the con."

"Ah." Royston nodded, but then looked puzzled once more. "But, they can't do that! Surely. They can't just leave us here to die. I refuse to believe it."

Tamara sighed. "They're criminals, pal. We don't know what they were here for, so goodness knows what they're capable of."

Royston blinked at her, realizing she was right, but wanting to believe otherwise.

One by one they sat down, trying to take in the finality of their predicament. They avoided looking one another in the eye, each with their own private thoughts.

After about twenty minutes, something caught Royston's eye. "Hey, look!" he cried, leaping up and pointing at the sky. "They're coming back!"

With rising hope, Buckman and Tamara got to their feet and looked where he was pointing. "That's not them," said Tamara, shaking her head.

"How can you tell?"

She turned to look at Royston as though he were an idiot. "Our ship was white. This one's pale blue."

"Good point," the pilot conceded. "Who do you think

it is, then?"

"The prison guards, coming to check on the escape?" suggested Buckman. "Or the next delivery of convicts?"

But Tamara was deep in thought as she examined the nearing spacecraft. "I wonder ..." she mused.

"What?" asked Royston and Buckman simultaneously, a degree of desperation in their voices.

"Apart from the colour, it looks just like our ship."

"So?"

"Hedging their bets."

"Pardon?"

Tamara still seemed to be thinking her logic through. Then she turned to the two men. "Backup," she said, now seemingly convinced of her reasoning. "Look, imagine you're a criminal stuck here on this God forsaken planet with no means of escape. But you have a communicator capable of reaching out to inhabited planets. So, you decide to con some gullible alien species into building a spaceship to your design and bringing it here for you to make good your escape."

"Go on," urged Buckman. He glanced over at the spaceship which was now slowing its descent.

"But how reliable might this gullible alien species be? They might screw up, get lost, change their minds, whatever. So, you need a backup strategy."

Buckman was nodding his head, while Royston still looked lost. "So, they contacted more than one gullible species," said the captain setting off at speed towards the spaceship as it prepared to land.

"Where's he going?" asked Royston.

"To meet gullible species Number Two," answered Tamara, setting off to follow. "Come on – before he launches into a speech."

*

Through one of the ship's portholes Buckman could see three small alien heads bobbing up, down, and side to side as they jostled for their first glimpse of ET. Buckman knew just how they were feeling: the thrill of First Contact with an advanced civilisation – something that, for him, was rather wearing off.

He turned to the others as they approached. "Right, I'll be Brucie. You two can fight it out for Joanna Lumley and David Attenborough."

"What?" asked Tamara, blinking at him.

Royston was shaking his head. "The aliens won't have a clue who they are."

Buckman shrugged. "Maybe not. But let's just go with it." He grinned, thrusting his chin out as far as it would go, in the manner of Sir Bruce Forsyth.

Tamara seemed to grasp Buckman's intentions and put an arm on his shoulder to stop him. "Wait, we can't just …" The sound of the spaceship door swishing open interrupted her. They turned to see three aliens, dressed in bright pink spacesuits, stepping out onto the planet's soil. Their manner of movement seemed nervous and timid. They kept glancing at one another as they took each uncertain step forward. One was trying to hide a flagpole behind its back, as though too embarrassed to be seen with it.

Before either Tamara or Royston could stop him, Buckman had stepped forward to greet the creatures with a wide grin. "Nice to see you, to see you nice." It was not at all a bad impression. The aliens, startled at first, soon relaxed and made some strange and complicated hand signals in return. Buckman reached into his pocket and pulled out the silver plaque. "No one goes away empty-handed." He thrust the plaque into the lead alien's hands. "Everyone's a winner, if you play your cards right." He searched his mind for more of Bruce Forsyth's catchphrases.

The moment the alien's eyes settled on the plaque, they lit up with excitement. It jabbered to the others, passing the plaque first to one and then the other. They conversed amongst themselves for a while before appearing to jabber words of gratitude towards the captain.

Buckman gave Tamara and Royston a victorious wink. "I knew it would come in handy."

Then, gently, he took the lead alien's elbow and guided it, and its companions, towards a patch of ground about 20 paces from the spaceship. He signalled to the one with the flagpole to insert it into the ground, which it did with much effort.

The little creatures commenced snapping pictures of themselves and their surroundings, like overenthusiastic tourists. Buckman pointed at one of their cameras and gave the universal sign for taking a picture. Camera in hand, he backed away towards the spaceship, as though trying to capture the perfect shot. "Right, here's the plan," he whispered to his crew. "When I say 'Go', you two make for the control room. Roy, start the engines. The moment I'm in, blast off." He waved to the aliens who remained stock still in their chosen poses next to the flag. "Say 'cheese', my loves."

"Are you crazy?" hissed Tamara. "We can't just steal their ship."

"Life ..." Buckman sang in Bruce Forsyth's voice. "... is the name of the game."

Tamara rolled her eyes.

"The captain's right," said Royston. "It us or them. There'll only be room for three in there."

Tamara uttered a horrified squeak. "Apart from anything else, we don't even know if the air in there is breathable, or the food edible. Have you thought of that?"

Buckman obviously hadn't; his entire being betrayed the fact. Clearing his throat, he said, "Er, good point. Very good point." He took a step towards the group of aliens and snapped another picture. "What do we do?"

Royston tapped him on the shoulder. "Look! Up there." He pointed up at the sky where another spaceship was approaching.

"Could it be Brucie?" asked Buckman, ever hopeful.

"It's not our ship," said Royston. "Ours didn't have those patterns."

"Gullible species Number Three," put in Tamara.

"And another." Royston swung his pointing finger to another approaching ship.

"Number Four."

"Blimey," said Buckman. "It seems Brucie and Co conned half the sentient beings in the Galaxy to come spring them from prison. Hats off to them." He turned to Tamara. "OK, this is what we do. I'll distract them with these new spaceships, and you go in there and check the air."

She grimaced, but then nodded. "OK."

Buckman strode over to the aliens and returned their camera, letting them look at the pictures he'd taken. There was much jabbering and giggling. Then he indicated the approaching ships and encouraging them to wave and take more pictures. The pink-suited aliens were only too glad to do so.

From the corner of his eye he saw Tamara re-emerging

from the spaceship, so he hurried over.

She was shaking her head. "Toxic air. Poisonous food."

"Damn!"

Royston emerged also. "I'd say they have some pretty disgusting personal habits. You do not want to know what's in there."

Buckman gave a deep sigh, before looking up at the approaching spacecraft in the sky. He checked his oxygen gauge. "We have an hour of air left." The others checked their gauges. "So, I guess it's Plan B."

"Which is?" asked both Tamara and Royston.

"We use our charm to make ourselves some new alien friends. Fast. And see if any of them can give us a lift home."

"Charm?" asked Royston with a splutter. "Good luck with that, then."

But Buckman had already returned to the group of pink-suited aliens and was gesticulating to them that he wanted the plaque back. After a few moments of remonstration, and a bit of a scuffle, he held the plaque aloft in triumph for Tamara and Royston to see, before heading off towards the first of the newly landed spaceships.

We're Back!

Although outlawed in every star system in the Galaxy, the savage sport of Gr'Uth flourished for tens of millions of years. Vast fortunes hinged on each contest: a battle to the death between two alien armies, each abducted from its home world and bred for intelligence, speed and aggression. The venues were remote and barren planets, their location secret until shortly before each fight. Many of the battles were long, brutal and horrific, with pitifully few survivors.

Eventually, the galactic authorities clamped down on the sport, rounding up and imprisoning the fight organizers, breeders and trainers. More problematic was the question of what to do with the abducted alien species. A programme of repatriation to their home worlds was seen as the only fair solution, returning them from whence they had come.

And so it was that, one chilly April morning, the good folk of Affpuddle, Dorset, woke to find their village besieged by ten thousand repatriated, super-evolved, lightning-fast, battle hardened T-rexes, hungry and mean – keen to retake their planet, and once more to rule it as its apex predators.

Bad Call

This story originally appeared as A Disastrous Decision in the Cogwheel Press anthology, A Turn of the Wheel

We all make mistakes, of course we do. From small slips to major blunders. However, seldom has anyone made a misjudgement of the magnitude that Tim made that night. To be fair, it was late and a bit spur-of-the-moment. Nevertheless, it would have calamitous consequences for the future of Humankind.

It was 3am when a bright flash of light and a roar like thunder jolted Tim from his sleep. He looked up to find himself staring at a large gaping hole in the wall where his bedroom window had been, and at two strange silhouettes climbing in.

He gulped and shot under the duvet, stopping all breathing and movement. Only his heart and mind raced. What was happening? Could it be a prank? College mates, perhaps? But the figures had been too short to be any of his friends in costume. And what the blazes had happened to the window?

Tim stiffened at the sound of the figures approaching his bed. Then he heard a burbly, sing-song noise, which turned out to be speech. "Hello there, little human-human."

Tim's eyes widened under the cover, but apart from that he didn't move.

"We are Thereem and we come in peace-peace," continued the burbling voice. "Sort of-of."

This last statement caught Tim's attention. Tentatively he surfaced and poked an eye over the bedcovers.

"Sort of?" he asked with a frown. He surveyed the two short aliens in the weird glow that filled the room. The creatures had thick necks, short, stubby legs, long snaking arms, and what looked like a beer gut. Each had two independently wandering eyes that surveyed the room and would occasionally flick in Tim's direction. The only positive to be taken from the situation was that they didn't appear to be armed. "What do you mean: you come in peace, 'sort of'?"

The aliens looked at one another and made a noise like a girlish giggle.

"Our intentions are largely friendly-friendly." The shorter of the two was the one doing all the talking.

"Largely?" queried Tim, sitting up.

"Indeed. Come with us-us."

"No way. Who are you?"

"I already said. We are Thereem. I am Zablik and this is Thrbok-Thrbok."

"The Ream?"

Zablik seemed to sigh impatiently. "It is pronounced 'Thereem-Thereem'."

"Thereme-Thereme," tried Tim.

"No, no, no. You're getting it all wrong. First, there is only one 'Thereem', not two. And secondly, it is pronounced 'Thereem'. Put your tongue to the roof of your mouth. Like this: Thereem-Thereem."

"You keep saying two The Reems."

The taller alien, Thrbok, who had not yet spoken, raised a snaking arm to his mouth and leaned towards Tim before whispering, "Zablik has a speech impediment. Please ignore it as he is very sensitive about it."

Zablik swivelled to face Thrbok. "Speech impediment? How dare you-you? I have no speech impediment-impediment."

Tim said nothing, thinking it best to stay out of it. He gave the name another try, "Threem."

"Hah!" said Zablik triumphantly, pointing at Tim. "Now that's what I call a speech impediment-impediment." The jelly-like protuberances on his head wobbled wildly. "Anyway, we have no time to waste. You must come with us now-now."

"Is this an alien abduction?" Tim shrank back, pulling the duvet up to his chin.

"No," said Thrbok. "It's an alien rescue. We have come to save your species."

Tim raised an eyebrow. "Save my species? From what?"

The Thereem burbled to one another for a few seconds.

"Well?" prompted Tim.

"Er," started Thrbok, his eyes flicking this way and that, avoiding Tim's gaze. "There's a … black hole. And it's … er … heading towards the centre of your planet."

"A black hole?"

Thrbok nodded. "As it falls, it will suck in the Earth. We estimate there are two of your Earth hours left before the crust caves in, and everything … and everyone … gets swallowed up by it."

Tim was at a loss for words. "But..."

"You must get ready for escape-escape."

"This doesn't make sense. Where did this black hole come from?"

"Ah," said Thrbok.

"Erm-erm," said Zablik.

Tim threw back the duvet cover and swung his legs to the floor. His eyes narrowed as he glared at the two aliens. "Did you guys have anything to do with this?"

"Ah," repeated Thrbok.

"Erm-erm," repeated Zablik.

"Well?"

"You are a creature of limited intelligence. We would not expect you to understand," said Thrbok.

"Try me."

Thrbok's eyes crossed and uncrossed. "Well, a couple of weeks ago we … er … borrowed a spaceship. How were we to know it was a black hole transporter – with a black hole loaded? Anyway, as we were making a tight turn through your planetary system the black hole, kind of, slipped out. Most unfortunate."

"I'd say so. That's how you define 'largely friendly,' is it? Dumping a black hole into the centre of our planet?"

"We all make mistakes," said Thrbok with a shrug.

"But at least we plan to make good our error. We are here to save your species."

Zablik stepped forward. "And we must act fast as we only have two hours left-left."

Tim glanced at his bedside clock. "How are you going to save everyone in two hours?"

The aliens exchanged glances. "We're not-not," said Zablik. "Not *everyone*. Like we said, we're going to save your species, but there's not enough room in our craft for everyone on this planet-planet."

Thrbok gave a solemn nod. "We can only take so many."

Tim's eyes narrowed again. "How many?"

The aliens shuffled their feet.

"Well?"

"Seven," said Thrbok finally.

Tim gave an involuntary laugh before screaming, "Seven??"

"More than enough to keep the species going. You're our first. Aren't you the lucky one? We just need six more to go with you."

Tim stared at them, unable to say anything.

Thrbok stepped forward and swept an arm to indicate the house. "Who else lives in this domicile?"

Tim hardly heard the question, so Thrbok repeated it.

"My landlady – who's a total monster – and her poor, hen-pecked husband."

"Would you like us to save them?"

Tim choked. "Crikey, no." Then he corrected himself, "That's to say, they wouldn't be in my top six."

"Very well. Please select your top six. You will be the last of your species, so please choose fit and healthy individuals to maximize breeding and survival chances."

Zablik seemed suddenly agitated and pointed both his rubbery arms at Tim, burbling at Thrbok as he did so.

"Good point," said Thrbok before turning to Tim. "We should have asked before. Are you fertile?"

Tim blinked several times at the question. "Er, well, I should imagine so. I've never been tested."

Both Thrbok and Zablik peered closely at him. "Hmm," said the former. "No time for an anal probe. Pity. We'll just have to take your word for it."

Tim felt his nether regions contracting at the thought.

"But you'd better hurry," urged Thrbok.

"What?"

"Six others-others," Zablik reminded him.

"Yes, yes," said Tim. He gave his head a shake in an effort to focus. He reached for his mobile phone and scrolled down his list of contacts, stopping at the gorgeous Samantha. He hesitated. Dare he? He hardly knew her; didn't even have a picture of her for the icon. But she'd hardly been out of his thoughts for most of the past week. If he'd had a picture he would probably have spent all his time just gazing at it. They had hit it off instantly. Hadn't they?

"Hurry-hurry."

"OK, OK." Tim tapped Samantha's blank icon and waited, his heart suddenly thumping in his chest.

Two rings, three rings, four rings, and then a click.

"Hello?" said a sleepy voice on the other end. Tim's stomach gave a somersault.

"Hi, Samantha. Er, this is Tim. I don't know if you remember me. From the Freshers' party last Saturday night."

"Who?"

"Tim. Studying Chemistry. We chatted about …

various things. Sorry to disturb you at this hour, but there's a black hole heading towards the centre of the Earth and these two aliens called the Thereme ..."

"Thereem-Thereem," corrected Zablik.

"... Theream, have broken into my bedroom ..."

"What the hell?" croaked Samantha. "Is this some kind of joke? It's 3 o'clock in the morning!"

"I know, I know. It sounds crazy, but ..."

Just before he heard the click, Tim caught the word "Creep." It was like a knife to his heart.

"Well?" asked Thrbok.

"Technical hitch," said Tim, still hurting. The conversation had not gone well. Could he call again and try a different tack? His insides churned.

"Maybe we've got the wrong person-person," said Zablik, turning as though to leave.

"No, I'm good," said Tim, raising a hand to halt him. "I'll call Barry. He's my best mate and he'll round up two or three girls in no time. He has a talent. You'll see." Tim tapped Barry's leering icon.

The Thereem exchanged glances. "Perhaps we should have gone straight to Barry's place," said Thrbok.

"Agreed-agreed." Zablik nodded.

"I'm sorry, the person you are calling is not available," said the recorded voice on Tim's phone. "But if you ..." Tim killed the call and sighed in exasperation. He gulped as he sensed the aliens were about to move on. With a shaking finger he scrolled up and down his address book. Jenny? They'd broken up two months previously, but she might still have feelings for him. If only he still had feelings for her.

"Time's running out," pressed Thrbok.

"I know, I know." Tim scrolled once more through his

address list. Who else was there? Flora? Quite a nice girl, but she was studying abroad. Jane? No, he'd never really fancied Jane. Molly? No way.

Besides, who would believe his crazy story and come at such short notice?

There was a sound of movement on the ceiling above their heads. All three froze.

"My landlady!" whispered Tim. "She doesn't allow company after 10pm. I think she primarily means lady friends, but if she sees what you've done to her window, I expect she'll extend the ban to extra-terrestrials."

"Are you sure you wouldn't like her to come along with us? Save a lot of time and trouble."

"No way!" spluttered Tim, his eyes popping.

"Why not-not?"

"Er, ..." Tim's mind raced. "She's not ... er ... not fertile. At least, I sincerely hope not."

"Must push you, then-then," hissed Zablik.

"Alright, alright."

It was at that point that Tim made the biggest, most disastrous, most far-reaching mistake of his entire life.

He phoned his mum. And his mum, being his mum, took control.

*

And so it was that Tim now found himself in an alien spaceship, fleeing a collapsing, crumbling Earth far below, his heart aching at thoughts of the fair Samantha, down there, being sucked into a ravenous black hole, and soon to be crushed out of existence – abandoned to her ghastly fate along with seven billion other people.

He thought fleetingly of Barry, too, but more about what might have been had he answered the phone, than about the guy himself.

Instead, here he was – one of the last seven surviving members of his species. He looked around at the others: his mum, his step-dad, granddad Alf, Great Aunt Agatha, old Bert from the pub and last, but not least, Rosie Scroggins, his mum's best friend from the Bingo Club.

Tim could not imagine what his mum had been thinking when she had assembled this lot, but propagation of the human race could not have been uppermost in her mind. Or, if it had ...

Tim shuddered.

Humankind was finished and he no longer cared.

Farther Christmas

I expect there aren't many people in the world called Wrzesław Gyurcsó, and certainly not in Catford. So it didn't take long for the secret service agents to find me.

There were two of them outside when I answered the front door. I could see their oversized footprints in the snow where they had plodded up the path after leaving the gate wide open. Not a stealth operation, then. The older man flashed me his ID card and introduced himself in a stern manner.

"Agent Wabbit of MI5. This is my colleague, Agent Grant." He glanced at the smartphone he was carrying before focusing his sceptical countenance on me. "Are you Mr Gurko?"

"Gyurcsó."

"Uh-huh?" he said, as though not entirely believing me. He checked the phone again and his lips tightened. "Mr W…" he tried, but gave up and showed me the name instead.

"Wrzesław Gyurcsó. Yes, that's me."

"Unusual name."

"Polish-Hungarian."

His eyes narrowed. "Is it?" He turned to Grant whose mind seemed to be elsewhere. "Did you get that?"

Grant started out of his trance and gave what was a blatant lie. "Yes, sir."

Agent Wabbit's face darkened as he turned back to me. "Now then, sir. We'd like to ask you a few questions on a matter of national security. May we come in?"

I found myself shaking a little. "Of c-course," I stammered before ushering them in. They stamped their boots on the doormat, although nowhere near enough to get rid of all the snow. "This way, Agent … er … Wabbit?"

He gave me a hostile stare. "Some people assume it must be Rabbit, and that I can't pronounce my Rs. I find that most annoying."

I dared not say a word, but merely indicated the living room.

Wabbit settled himself in the armchair next to the Christmas tree, while I sat on the sofa opposite, and Agent Grant took out a notebook and remained standing. He looked a little lost – as though he were a work experience student on his first day in the job. I noted he was standing underneath the mistletoe, which I hoped was not a deliberate act.

Wabbit stared at me for a full minute without saying a word. It made me feel instantly guilty of whatever crime or misdemeanour they had come to question me about. I glanced at Grant, but he seemed lost in thought once more.

Finally, Wabbit stroked his chin, still staring at me, and said, "This is a most unusual case, Mr Gurko. Most unusual." He glanced up at Grant who had noticed the mistletoe and was gazing up at it with a thoughtful expression. Wabbit cleared his throat with great exaggeration. "Er, Agent Grant. Would you mind observing Mr Gurko's reactions while under questioning?"

Grant pulled himself together. "Er, yes, sir. Of course, sir. Right away, sir." And then he, too, started staring at me.

Not only was I now under the twin beams of their observation, but Wabbit leaned forward to get a closer look. Observing every micro expression on my face, he asked, "What would it mean to you, sir, if I said: 'Merry Christmas'?"

I blinked in puzzlement, glancing up at Grant, and then back to Wabbit. Was this a joke, or a very cunning interrogation technique? "Well, Agent Wabbit, I would think that very sweet of you. Merry Christmas to you, too."

Wabbit gave a wry grin and cocked an eyebrow. I felt he was waiting for more reaction from me, but I was unable to supply any.

Wabbit's lips tightened and he eyed me with renewed determination, as though dealing with a particularly devious adversary. "Alright, then. Let's try this. Resedon.

What does Resedon mean to you?"

I pursed my lips and shook my head. "Nothing."

Wabbit looked up at Grant. "What do you think, Agent Grant? Are his reactions genuine?"

Grant swallowed hard, and his eyes widened in panic. He peered more closely at me. "Hmm," he said in what he must have presumed was a thoughtful manner. "Difficult to say."

Wabbit nodded. "For once, I agree with you." He leaned back on the sofa and looked down at his phone. "Better call the expert."

He located a number and punched it, watching me curiously as the phone rang. "Hello? Professor Fowler? Agent Wabbit here. Yes, I'm fine, thank you. Now, madam, we have located the suspect ... er, I mean subject of interest, and managed to speak to him. At first sight, he seems ... normal. Human, even."

I wasn't sure how to take that.

Wabbit continued, "No reaction when I said 'Merry Christmas'. Nor did he flinch when I mentioned the Resedon. Yes, that's right. Yes, yes. Of course." He put the phone on speaker mode and handed it to me. "She says she wants to speak to you."

I took the phone from him as though it was a stolen item, glancing uncertainly at both men as I held it in my palm.

"Hello?" said the voice on the line. "Is that Wrzesław Gyurcsó?"

I perked up in surprise. "Your pronunciation's very good."

The voice chuckled. "I've been practising. We have a Polish postdoc and a Hungarian intern in the lab who have been training me. My name's Emma. Have you heard of SETI?"

"No."

"It stands for the Search for Extra Terrestrial Intelligence. We use spare time on the world's radio and other telescopes to search for signals that could be messages from aliens. I'm in charge of the SETI unit here at Jodrell Bank."

Wabbit was watching my every move, so he must have detected the waves of utter bewilderment radiating from me.

"We've picked up a signal from Epsilon Eridani b," Emma was saying, "It's an extrasolar planet about 10.5 light years away. It took a while to decode the message, but we think we've finally cracked it."

I had to cut in. "Can I just stop you there? I think there's been some kind of mistake. I can't see how this has any relevance to me."

"Ha!" exclaimed Wabbit, while Grant snorted.

"Yes, sorry," came Emma's lilting voice from the phone. "This must all seem rather strange to you, but I think you'll find it's even odder when you hear the next part."

"Go on."

"So, the message we decoded is: 'Merry Christmas' …"

My eyebrows rose.

"… and it's addressed to *you*."

My eyebrows could go no higher, so my mouth dropped open instead. "What?"

"The message is addressed to Wrzesław Gyurcsó of Catford. It is signed: 'The Resedon'."

"Must be some kind of prank."

"Our first thought, too, Wrzesław. But we've checked

and rechecked the readings, replicated the observations, tried other decodings."

I was shaking my head. "No, come on. That can't be right. For one thing, why would extra-terrestrials be sending Christmas greetings from 10.5 light years away, and, for another, why to me? Of all the people on Earth, why me?"

"That's what Agent Wabbit is there to find out."

I glanced at Wabbit and he gave me a humourless smile. I looked back at the phone. "Can I see the message?"

"Sure," said Emma. "Roger?"

For a moment, I thought she was indicating she had understood my meaning, until it slowly dawned on me that she was addressing Agent Wabbit by his first name. I tried to disguise the huge grin that was threatening to spread across my face.

Wabbit gave an embarrassed cough before snapping his fingers at his junior. "Grant. Show him the message."

Agent Grant flicked through his notebook until he came to the right page. He handed it to me.

"WRZESLAWGYURCSOOFCATFORDMERRYXMASTHERESEDON."

I stared at the message for a full minute. Then, suddenly, a chill ran down my spine. My throat constricted and my heart started pounding. I glanced up at Wabbit and there was no way he could have missed the look of horror on my face.

"Aha-ha!" he exclaimed, clapping his hands in triumph. "We have a reaction, Professor. We have a definite reaction."

We certainly had a reaction. I'd had an idea that might explain everything. I cleared my throat. "Professor

Fowler …"

"Please call me Emma."

"Emma. Could I send a reply?"

Wabbit stiffened, and Grant took a step back.

"Er, well," came the voice on the phone. "We could try. Sure. What's the message?"

"*Love you always.*"

"What?" said both Emma and Wabbit simultaneously. Grant snatched back his notebook and jotted down a hurried note.

"Just that," I said. "*Love you always.*"

"What's the significance of that?" asked the professor's anxious voice. "Have you worked out the meaning of the original message?"

"Yes, I think I have."

"What is it?"

I handed the phone back to Wabbit. "If I'm right, this closes a Missing Persons case for the police."

Wabbit sat back, dumbfounded. "Missing Persons?"

"The message isn't signed 'The Resedon', but 'Thérèse Don'. She was my fiancée. Disappeared on Christmas Eve, 1982. We were planning to tell our parents of our engagement the following day. But she never showed. Vanished. No trace of her was ever found. She's sent 'Merry Christmas' so I would know it's from her."

Wabbit was as baffled as I had been earlier, but the professor had caught up with me. "You think she was abducted by aliens?"

"I guess so. And the message shows she's alive and well."

Wabbit was in a turmoil of incomprehension. "What? Where? So where is she?"

"Epsilon Eridani b," put in Emma. "10.5 light years away."

I felt the emotions flooding over me once more. "Now, if you can excuse me, I think I need to go and have a cry."

Agent Grant took a handkerchief from his pocket and offered it to me.

I declined it.

The Knowledge Drain

A version of this story originally appeared as Appendix III in The Ultimate Inferior Beings by Mark Roman

The wormids were unique among all alien species in having achieved the ultimate goal of any advanced civilization: they knew Everything.

They had discovered everything there was to discover, proved everything there was to be proven, invented everything there was to be invented, and learned everything there was to be learnt.

There was nothing they didn't know, nothing they

didn't understand, and no mysteries left to solve. The Universe no longer held, nor could hold, any secrets for them.

Or, at least, that was what they thought ...

*

Pfnug the Hodeus sat staring through his spaceship's control-room window, hoping for some ugliness among the stars streaming towards him. He needed to find something really, really ugly and he needed to find it really, really fast. Time was running out.

He sighed a nervous sigh as his thoughts turned to his principal rival, Dork. He had to beat Dork to win Chella. But Dork was good. *Really* good. A shudder passed through Pfnug's bloated, semi-transparent body, setting off a series of throbs and wet pulsations, and causing various gases and stenches to be emitted. He scratched his sagging face, covered in boils, warts, patches of sliminess, areas of hairiness, and regions of mouldiness. One could not call Pfnug a handsome Hodeus. But then again, there was no such thing as a handsome Hodeus. All Hodei were, not to put too fine a point on it, repulsive – a survival strategy evolved and perfected over many millennia. The uglier and more repellent a Hodeus, the less likely it was to be eaten by the hungry predators on Slokkit. This, in turn, made the Hodei rather solitary creatures, for no Hodeus could stand the sight, sound nor smell of any other Hodeus. As for the other two senses – touch and taste – no two Hodei ever came close enough to experience such horrors. This was the stuff of Hodeus nightmares. (For the reader's benefit, the delicate matter of how Hodei reproduced will not be described here).

Pfnug glanced at the mirror on the wall to his right. "I am so ugly," he muttered, and felt immediately reassured.

His internal and external organs rumbled and squeaked and hissed, causing a darkish cloud of foul-looking, and fouler-smelling, fumes to engulf him and fill him with confidence. "I can do this!" he squeaked. "I know I can."

*

The three little wormids stood in silence in their little craft, watching the stars before them. Their craft was one of a vast flotilla of widely-dispersed wormid ships speeding away from their home planet, heading to a new beginning, a new future. The wormids knew exactly where they were, exactly where they were going and exactly how long it would take to get there.

Each had a knowledgeable, and perhaps slightly smug, look on its face. No words were exchanged, for there was no need to speak; conversation was unnecessary and redundant, and, in fact, quite annoying.

Names, too, were not needed as all wormids looked the same, did the same things, and even thought the same thoughts.

*

As Pfnug adjusted a couple of his external organs in the mirror to present them in a more revolting aspect, he spotted something out of the corner of his rheumy, bulging eyes. A faint signal on one of the scanners. His three hearts missed a beat. Ramping up detector sensitivity, the signal became clearer. Another spaceship. In his excitement, his guts squirted liquid in all directions. His face turned from red to purple to blue-green and then to orange.

"Yesss!" he hissed. "This is it."

He took hold of the controls and headed towards the spot of light, just visible through the window in front of him.

"I see it, I see it!" he shrieked in his grating, high-pitched squeak.

It looked small; a small sphere, with several bent tubes coming radially out of it, like twigless branches. It wasn't obviously ugly. In fact, it merely looked ridiculous and impractical. But ugly? He peered at it more closely, unsure. Could it be made more unpleasant on the eye? Perhaps under the right lighting conditions?

As he dithered uncertainly, one of his organs voided itself of its foul contents.

*

The wormids stared proudly and haughtily out of the window ahead of them. They were proud to be wormids. Proud of their ancestors, proud of their fellow wormids and, above all, proud of themselves.

But things were about to change.

A small spot of light appeared far off to the left of their field of view, and gradually grew. At first, it didn't register, as it wasn't something they were expecting to see. But the light kept growing. And, once it had grown into a large, brightly-lit, ugly-looking object filling most of their field of view, they could no longer fail to be aware of it.

They shuffled uneasily. One by one, each wormid shot a haughty glance at the others to see if they were also aware of the object. But all they got were equally haughty glances back. Their eyes returned to the uncomfortable sight before them and the tension in the little craft mounted.

When the object was filling their entire window, the one in the middle could stand it no longer and spoke. It was the first time a wormid had opened his mouth in a very long time. "I knew this would happen," he said, looking down his nose at the other two and nodding his head towards the object in the window. "I knew it."

"So did I," said the one on the right with equal snootiness.

"Me too," said the third.

The three wormids threw contemptuous looks at one another before turning back to the object. They knew the others were lying.

But then, they knew Everything.

*

Pfnug was still a ball of confusion and uncertainty. Was the thing ugly enough to win? Beads of sweat appeared on his forehead.

He leaned out of his seat and took a deep slurp of the revolting bodily fluids that had pooled on the floor around him. This always made him feel better. One of his stomachs burbled loudly, which made him feel better still.

And then, as he looked back at the object floating in space in front of his ship, he spewed up a copious quantity of green slime. This made him feel best of all.

*

The first wormid who had spoken, slightly taller than the others, broke the silence once again. "Do you suppose the others know of this?"

The one on his right, who was middle in size and female, replied, "Of course they know."

"I know," said the short one, nodding.

Silence.

"I bet they don't," said Tall suddenly.

The Medium and Short wormids swung around in horror as though Tall had just uttered the ultimate blasphemy (which, in wormid terms, he had). They glared at him.

"I bet they don't know," repeated Tall. "You know I'm right."

All three wormids looked slightly embarrassed, not knowing what to say or do. And the fact they didn't know what to say or do only compounded their embarrassment.

Eventually, Tall said, "Are you thinking what I'm thinking?"

Medium gave a derisive snort. "Of course," she said.

Short also snorted. "Of course," he said.

"Very well," said Tall. "There's no other course of action."

"We realize that," said the others.

"So, who's going to do it?"

"I will," said Short. He sidled up to the steering wheel and turned it as far to the right as it would go. The craft veered to the right and, a short while later, the vast and ugly object was no longer visible. He stepped back with a self-satisfied smirk.

The other two were staring at him in astonishment.

"What did you do that for?" asked Tall.

"We'd agreed I would."

"No. We agreed that there was only one course of action and that you would carry it out."

"Which I did."

Tall was shaking his head. "But that wasn't it!"

Medium agreed with him. "He's right, it wasn't."

Short looked at them, puzzled. "Yes, it was."

"Nope," said Tall, shaking his head.

"Nope," agreed Medium.

"Look, if that's what I had been thinking," pursued Short, "you two must have been thinking the same thing!"

"Not me," said Tall.

"Nor me," said Medium.

Short looked baffled. "Alright, then, what had you been thinking?"

"That we should destroy the object," said Tall.

Medium swung towards him. "No," she said. "I had been thinking we should let the other wormid ships know."

All three mouths dropped open and the wormids started shaking in fright and shock.

They were no longer thinking the same thoughts! This could mean only one thing: that they no longer knew Everything.

*

Pfnug woke to find himself lying on the floor in the pool of his noxious juices. In his excitement, he must have fallen asleep and slipped off his seat. His throat felt dry and swollen, while his mouth tasted of something indescribable. Leaning down to the floor, he took another quick slurp of the vile liquid, but this time it made him feel quite sick.

"Blyeuhh!" he spluttered as he spat the liquid out.

Groaning in pain, Pfnug picked himself off the floor and dropped back into his seat with an almighty squelch. There, before him, was the strange little space object, now floating some distance away. His thoughts turned to Chella.

"Ah, Chella," he murmured with a sigh. "Sweet, revolting, gentle Chella."

The thoughts jerked him into activity. If he wanted to win Chella, this object might be his only hope. He'd have to grab it fast and speed back to Slokkit. There wasn't much time. If he acted quickly, Chella could be his forever.

*

"What should we tell the others?" asked Tall.

"We don't know," responded Medium and Short. Three little words they had never dreamt they would ever use. They blinked in horror at one another.

"Wait," said Tall as a thought struck him. "I've had a thought."

The others looked startled, for no thought had struck them at the same time.

"I bet it's that object. That's what's doing it."

The others looked baffled, not having a clue what Tall was talking about. But, being too proud to admit it, they said nothing.

"It's a Knowledge Drain," continued Tall.

"A what??"

"Look. Everything was alright until that thing came along. We knew Everything. Right?"

The others gave impatient but slightly sceptical nods.

"We had discovered all the Universe's secrets and possessed all the Knowledge there was to possess. And then ...," he nodded his head at the vast, ugly object which was once again in full view at their window, "... that thing showed up."

"Get on with it," said Medium.

"So, it stands to reason it must have drained our knowledge somehow. It must be a Knowledge Drain."

"What nonsense," scoffed Medium.

"I've never heard such rot," said Short with undisguised disdain.

"It's the only possible explanation," insisted Tall.

"Prove it!" said Medium and Short together.

THE KNOWLDEGE DRAIN

*

Wasting no time, Pfnug worked the controls of his spaceship to manoeuvre it towards the object. As his ship approached, he opened the hold bay door and prepared to let the hold swallow the small thing up ...

*

"I just know I'm right," said Tall with all the conviction he could muster.

"And we just know you're wrong," said Medium with a sweet smile.

"Alright, what's *your* explanation?"

Medium suddenly looked very sad. "Perhaps we never really knew Everything in the first place. Simple as that."

Tall gave her a horror-stricken look. He turned to Short. "What's *your* take? Did we have Total Knowledge, or didn't we?"

"Dunno," said Short with a shrug.

Medium was shaking her head. "Look," she said, "if we really knew Everything, we'd have known about this 'Knowledge Drain' and would have avoided it."

"Good point," said Tall.

"Thank you."

"But I'm one step ahead of you. Let me explain. Say we knew of the Knowledge Drain's existence, but *didn't* avoid it? Say we deliberately sought it out. We knew what we were doing and had a very good reason for doing it. After all, we knew Everything."

Medium didn't look convinced, while Short merely looked confused. "How can you 'drain' knowledge?" he asked.

"Good question," said Tall. "But you should have asked me about an hour ago when I would have known the answer." He flashed Short a false smile

Short smiled falsely back. "I would have known the answer myself then, wouldn't I."

"So you would," said Tall, his smile even falser than before. "So you would."

The two of them continued to try to out-smile one another until Medium interrupted them. "So, what are we going to do?"

"Get our knowledge back!" cried Tall as though it were the most obvious thing in the world. "We go inside that object and retrieve it."

Medium laughed. But, as she did so, her eyes caught sight of the black gap that was opening in the object outside. The others turned to see why her mouth had suddenly dropped open. The black gap was getting larger and larger because they were moving towards it.

"There, see?" said Tall. "We're going inside." He gulped.

Their craft was now inside the object. A quick glance through the back window only confirmed their fears. The panel that had opened to let them in was now closing. Their craft was in total darkness. They were trapped.

All three wormids swallowed nervously.

"Right," said Tall, trying to hide the shakiness in his voice. "We're in. Phase One accomplished." He looked at the worried expressions on his companions' faces, lit eerily by the small lamps in their spacecraft's control room. "Now all we've got to do is go out there and get our knowledge back."

*

With the small object securely stored in the hold, Pfnug set the ship's course for Slokkit. Full speed.

As the ship sped through space, he sat gnawing his

bloated lower lip in an agony of doubt, worrying about the object. Was it ugly enough to win Chella? Would it beat Dork's entry?

He sweated and fretted and stewed in his fetid juices. It was no good. He had to take a closer look. Perhaps it would look uglier close up.

With his three hearts pounding, he slid off his seat with a splash and waded through the lake of bodily fluids to the door. As he opened it, the liquids gushed out into the corridor. He followed them towards the spiral staircase leading down into the hold area.

Entering the hold, he switched on the lights and, in trepidation, approached the object. He leaned his repulsive, bloated, glutinous mass over it and peered in through a little window in the side.

Within the object, three little creatures squirmed a little before raising half their length upright.

"Wow," exclaimed Pfnug, puffing out with joy. "They're aliens! Ugly little buggers, too."

He burst out laughing. "They are so ugly! Absolutely hideous. Yuk." He stood grinning from one side of his bloated head to the other.

"Chella's as good as mine," he roared and did a little dance. "Dork will never come up with anything as horrible as these!"

Still laughing, Pfnug left the hold.

*

"What the heck was that?!?" asked Short.

"I don't know," said Tall. "But I'm glad it's gone."

"That was the most repulsive thing I've ever seen," said Short with a shudder. The others shuddered in agreement.

"It left a terrible mess behind," said Medium,

indicating the steaming pools of foul fluid that remained around their spaceship.

"Indeed," said Tall, but he had hardly heard what she had said. He was busy scanning the place for any signs of knowledge. "Right, I guess we'd better go out and start searching this place. Time's running out. We don't have long before the Light goes ..."

"Yes, yes, I know," said Short. "But there's no way I'm going out there. No way. No, siree. Not with that thing on the loose."

"Me neither," said Medium. "You're on your own, buddy."

Tall gave them a disappointed look. "Very well, then ..." he started. But as he set off towards the exit his eyes caught the pools of foul fluid outside, and he stopped. "OK, maybe later."

*

Back in his control room, Pfnug was still chuckling to himself. "Dork was right," he was saying. "I was right. We were both right."

He leaned down and noisily slurped some liquid off the floor.

"Yeeuuhh!" he said with a grimace, allowing most of it to dribble back out of his mouth. "We both knew we had plundered all the ugly things to be found on Slokkit. Space was the answer. There'd be far more hideous things out here in space. So, we built our ships, Dork and I. The others, of course, copied us.

"And we were right! Except that Dork doesn't know it, yet!!" He laughed as he reflected on the three creatures down in his hold. "Wow. They're the most nauseatingly disgusting things I have ever seen in my life!"

He leaned back in his seat and thought sweet thoughts

about Chella and how she would very soon be his.

*

Tall pressed his head against the window to check that the alien wasn't hiding just out of sight.

"That big, wet, repulsive thing," Tall said. "I bet that's what took our knowledge."

Medium rolled her eyes. "Do you," she said.

"I'm sure of it."

"What now?" asked Short.

"Wait until it comes back," said Tall.

"And then what?" asked Medium. "Pounce on it? Body search it? Rather you than me."

"That's not quite what I had in mind."

"What then?"

"I don't know," said Tall with a grimace. "But remember, we used to know Everything. So, we knew what we were doing in coming here. We knew we'd find a way through this somehow. We knew it."

*

Pfnug beamed and bounced about in his seat with joy, for he could see his home planet now, looming up ahead and getting larger and larger.

"Slokkit! Slokkit!" he cheered, eyes popping out. The closer his ship got, the greater his excitement, until his pulsating, wheezing, hissing body could take no more, and Pfnug once again lost consciousness, dropping off his seat with a loud splash.

*

The three wormids sensed that the spaceship carrying them had landed. A little while later they felt their craft being picked up and carried outside. Through the window they could see they were on a planet, and it was night time. They gazed up into the night sky to work out from the constellations where they were. It was not good news.

"You know where we are, don't you," said Tall.

"We do," confirmed the other two dolefully.

"We're back in the Light system," said Tall, deciding to spell it out for them anyway. "We've been taken back. Which means that, when the Light goes supernova in a few hours' time ... we'll go with it!"

"We know," said the other two wormids sadly. "We know."

*

"Next!" roared the Great Tuatt from a distance.

Pfnug the Hodeus came forward, holding his precious find in trembling hands, nervous both of dropping it and of its chances of winning the competition. He approached the podium and glanced uncertainly at the Great Tuatt who was safely situated several hundred yards away. With pounding hearts, Pfnug carefully placed the object on the podium. He turned it a little to present its ugliest face to the Great Tuatt.

Then, retracing his steps, he retreated until he was far enough away from the podium to enable the Great Tuatt to approach without being repulsed by Pfnug's presence. His lower limbs were shaking like jelly, and his forehead spouting sweat, as the tension became unbearable.

The Great Tuatt, with the solemn authority of a high-ranking Hodeus, slithered and squelched and hissed and burped his way over to the podium. He leaned down to peer more closely at the object on it. He noticed the window and looked inside. There he saw three tiny worm-like creatures jumping up and down. He shot a questioning look at the distant ugly figure of Pfnug, but

THE KNOWLDEGE DRAIN

Pfnug just smiled back revoltingly. The Great Tuatt turned to the three, jumping worm-things, wondering not only what they were, but also why they were jumping up and down like that.

There seemed to be a pattern and rhythm to their leaps. At each one, they would nod their heads in the same direction. The Great Tuatt looked in the direction they were indicating, but all he could see was the Lumen, the star about which Slokkit orbited.

Jump, nod. Jump, nod.

"Hmm," said the Great Tuatt. He noticed also that, at each jump, the three worm-things emitted a high-pitched squeaking noise. He had assumed it to be one of his stomachs, but now he realized the noise to be coming from the worm-things.

Jump, nod, squeak. Jump, nod, squeak. Jump, nod, squeak.

The Great Tuatt made a revolting noise in his throat, straightened up, and looked at Pfnug in the distance.

"Repugnant!" he called out before stepping back the full hundred yards to his original position. "Next!"

*

The three wormids, hoarse and exhausted from all their screaming and jumping, lay on the floor of their spacecraft, frustrated, demoralized and sick.

"What is the matter with them?" asked Tall in exasperation.

"Why won't they listen?" asked Medium.

"They're spectacularly repulsive," said Short, as though that explained everything.

Tall sighed. "Any minute now …"

"… the Light will go supernova," finished Medium for him.

"And then we'll be toast," added Short.

One by one they groaned a long, weary, helpless groan.

Suddenly, Tall leapt up. "That's it!" he exclaimed. "I've got it! Now I know it all!"

"You do?" asked Medium, sitting up.

"Well no, not all," admitted Tall. "But I think I know why we encountered the Knowledge Drain."

Medium's face sagged, but she asked the question anyway. "OK, why did we encounter the 'Knowledge Drain'?"

"Self-sacrifice," said Tall.

"What are you on about?"

"Look, we knew Everything. We knew everything there was to know. We knew the Light was about to go supernova. We were leaving the Light system for a new future, a new beginning. But we also knew about the Knowledge Drain and what a danger it posed to us. We knew we would have to destroy it – before it destroyed us!"

Medium and Short were frowning deep frowns as Tall's theory unfolded.

"So, we three volunteered to encounter the Knowledge Drain. We must have known that it would first drain our knowledge, then capture us, and finally bring us here to its home planet. Once back here, we knew the supernova explosion would destroy the Knowledge Drain forever." Tall lowered his head before adding, "And us with it."

Medium and Short looked at him as though he were insane. He returned their looks with slow, solemn nods. "Yes," he said. "We three volunteered to sacrifice our lives so that the others could fly from the Light system to a new beginning – free from the threat of the Knowledge

THE KNOWLDEGE DRAIN

Drain."

The other two wormids continued to look at Tall as though he were insane, but now, despite everything, found themselves half-believing what he was saying. After all, it all seemed to fit. It had a warped logic to it and seemed to sort of make sense. Indeed, it seemed to provide their lives with some sort of purpose and meaning.

"Wasn't that noble of us," said Tall.

"Wasn't it," said Medium.

"Wasn't it," said Short.

*

Back home, in his underground lair, Pfnug had a little smile on his bloated face as he thought about the strange, ugly little object he had brought with him from space. He even hummed a little tune, a little tunelessly. Surely Chella was his.

Outside, he heard the sound of approaching squelches. He stiffened.

"Who is it?" he called.

"It's Frut," came a revolting, squeaky response. Pfnug shuddered at the sound of it. He didn't know any Hodeus called Frut, and nor did he want to.

"Why do you foul my ears with the sound of your vile voice?" yelled Pfnug up the passageway of his lair.

"Oh, what grotesque noise is that I hear?" came the response from outside. "And the stench that emanates from this hole is the most disgusting thing I have ever encountered!"

"Leave my path unfouled, you monstrous creature!"

The formalities over, Frut came to the point of his visit. "The judging is over, you vile excrescence. You came a pitiful second."

"How dare you insult me with your presence," cried Pfnug, trying desperately to hide the hurt in his voice. Second! He had lost again. No doubt about the winner, then.

"That foul, wretched stench that calls itself Dork won, I presume?" he called.

"Your conclusions are correct, even if your voice, your smell and your domicile disgust me," confirmed Frut.

Pfnug's lower, blubbery lip trembled in dismay. How had Dork found something more disgusting than his little worm things? He addressed the question to Frut.

Frut was so deeply offended by the way Pfnug had phrased the question that it took him a little while to compose himself and answer back. "That foul, wretched stench that calls itself Dork discovered an alien so foul that there is surely no equal anywhere in the Universe."

"How can that be?? What is this monstrous creature?"

"It has a vile name," answered Frut, choking on the smell coming from the entrance to Pfnug's home. "It called itself a humongbeyng."

Pfnug shuddered at the horror of these words. The name was indeed vile. Yet his curiosity got the better of him. However vile it was, he had to see it.

"Where is this monstrosity?" he called.

"Not here, thankfully. Dork was instructed to remove it so as not to pollute our land with its foulness. He took it in his spaceship back to its planet, Herth."

Pfnug shook his head in disappointment. It was all too much for him. He had lost again, and Dork had won. Life just wasn't fair.

He checked the calendar. The next competition was in a week's time. The prize: Rubimma.

Pfnug sighed. "Ah. Sweet, revolting, gentle

THE KNOWLDEGE DRAIN

Rubimma."

*

Tall, Medium and Short joined tails and gazed up at the screen in their little spaceship and watched as a digital clock counted down: 10, 9, 8 ...

They closed their eyes and braced themselves for the searing blast that was about to rip through their planetary system and burn everything to a crisp. Short uttered a whimper, Medium held her breath, and Tall faced the sky with the bravest look he could muster.

... 3, 2, 1, zero.

They waited.

And waited.

But nothing happened.

They turned to look at one another and blinked in puzzlement.

"Er," said Tall, checking the digital clock, now stopped at "0:00.00". "How do you explain that?"

"Interesting," said Medium.

"Hmm," said Short, scratching its chin in thought.

Medium looked out at the grey sky. "I wonder what the others will make of it. When they realize the Truth ..."

Short Shorts: 100-word stories

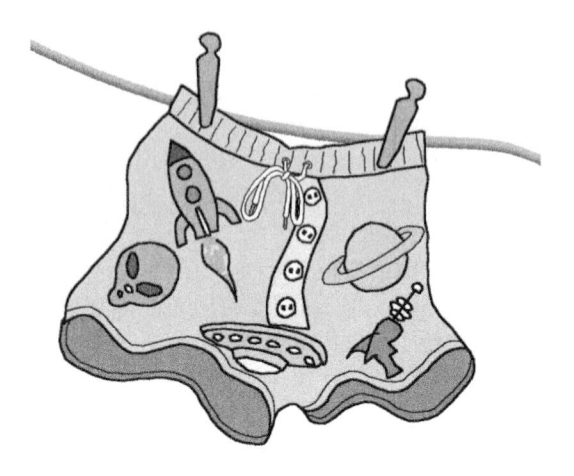

Dragon Slayer

"Tremble before me, ye vile monster," bellowed the golden knight, shaking his magnificent sword at the scaly beast towering above him. "For I am the mighty Sir Jasperot of Birhamham. Son of Grinklethor. Ruler of Midlandia. Slayer of dragons!"

The dragon gave a smirk and turned to examine its claws. "Name's Nigel," it hissed with barely a glance at the knight. Then, in a flurry of wings, flaming nostrils and a swishing tail, it swooped down from its perch and swallowed him whole. "Devourer of pretentious jerks," it added, with a burp, as it flew back to its lofty nest.

SHORT SHORTS

A Nice New Home

Better look sharp. Customers!

What've we got? Mum, dad, two kids. Promising.

Come here. Pick me! Get me outta this filthy tank; I'll be a faithful, loving pet.

Wow, they've chosen me, they've chosen me!

Journey's not much fun, but the house looks grand. Little girl's all smiles; we're gonna be great friends.

Mum's carrying me.

We're headed for a round, metal container. Doesn't look like a fish-tank. It contains water, but the water's bubbling and churning and steaming.

Something's not right. If only my claws weren't strapped shut.

Surely she's not going to ...

No. Wait!

You can't.

Noooooo!

The Magic Sword

Having mislaid his map, Sir Naylor the Negligent quickly became lost in the Cursed Forest and, after one wrong turn too many, blundered into the dreaded Quarry of Doom.

In an instant, a horde of evil demons surrounded him, their devilish eyes glowing, their sharp teeth glinting in the moonlight.

Only one thing could save Naylor the Negligent now:

his magic sword, Garethlor. Forged by elvish blacksmiths, engraved by dwarfish craftsmen, and enchanted by Merlin himself, it would make light work of these monstrous fiends.

It was a pity, then, that he'd left it on the kitchen table that morning...

And Then There Were ...

Three days on this nightmarish island, cut off from the world. Phone lines cut, no power, the castle in darkness. The boat's not due until Wednesday.

Four have been murdered so far, leaving just six. The barrister had her throat slit with a ceremonial sword; the dentist was drowned in the well; the bank manager was found hanging in the stairwell. And this morning, the doctor was poisoned. Screamed a long time before he passed away. Strychnine. Very nasty.

Terror grips everyone.

Who will be next?

No one knows who the killer is.

No one so much as suspects me.

Flies, Damned Flies, and Stacked Biscuits

Good day to you, I trust you are well. My name is Mr Benjamin Mbibi-yaya of Lagos, Nigeria, born in the year of our Lord 1993. I am an honest man living in a world of much dishonesty, as you will see from the story I am about to tell you.

Two weeks ago, I was visiting my late client's widow, Mrs Robinseki, to offer my condolences on the untimely death of her husband. She was busy with funeral arrangements at their splendid mansion. My emotions were mixed; it was a sad occasion for sure, but I was excited to see her. You see, I have a soft spot for the lady – and a bit of a hard spot, too, if you know what I am saying. A beautiful, beautiful woman, not so young these days, and with a much fuller figure than she used to have – but the kind of roundedness that I find most appealing.

Dressed in black, looking stunning, she stood with her arms open in welcome. All around her was the frenzied activity of personal assistants and servants hurrying this way and that. But the room was so dammed hot – a feature of my country in this age of global warming which I find does not suit me, especially when I am about to meet a lady as attractive as Mrs Robinseki.

I approached her, mopping the sweat from my brow and batting away a bothersome fly. I told her I was very sorry for her loss.

She took my hands in hers and gave them a warm squeeze. "Thank you, Benjamin. You are so sweet. But you know my husband was a very evil man."

I blinked, unsure what to say.

"Hobnob?" she asked, smiling sweetly as she handed me an open tin of the oat-based biscuits covered with a layer of thick, thick chocolate to which I am partial. I took the tin from her, and was about the select one when I noticed several flies had become trapped in the melting chocolate. "Damn those flies," I said to myself, disappointed at having to forego such a tasty treat.

Mrs Robinseki glanced around the room before beckoning me to follow her swaying and fulsome figure into a side office, away from the bustle. "Business," she whispered into my ear as I passed through the opening and she pushed the door shut.

A shiver of excitement shot through me as she seated us both on a sofa, me with the tin of Hobnobs on my lap. The very proximity of her voluptuous body stirred up feelings that contravened most of the rules taught by Bishop Barry Adebanjo. I was struggling with the heat of the situation, while the state of the Hobnobs was going from bad to worse.

She edged closer to me, taking one of my hands in hers. I gulped.

"My husband, Thomas," she started, "had a secret bank account …"

"Oh," I said, trying to hide the disappointment in my voice; she really did mean 'business'.

"… with a vast amount of illegal money in it. About 600 million US dollars."

I whistled.

"Now, you are a clever man ..."

I blushed under her intense gaze.

"… a graduate of Cambridge University!"

"Canbridge," I corrected her. It was a mistake I had also made when applying to this online college. It is now closed, for reasons that are not relevant here.

"I need your clever lawyer brain to find a way of getting at that money without alerting the Nigerian Tax Office."

"Ah," I said with a nod of understanding and rubbed my chin in thought. Another fly buzzed around the chocolate biscuits and I flapped a useless hand at it.

After a minute, I said, "Hmm. I would say we need someone with a foreign bank account. We transfer the funds there and the tax authorities are none the wiser."

Mrs Robinseki's eyes lit up and she clapped her hands. "I knew that, with your clever brain, you would find a way, Benjamin! Maybe one of your Cambridge friends?"

"Canbridge," I repeated, but didn't press the point. "Leave it with me."

"I will reward you most generously." She beamed at me and, as is her nature when in a good mood, she stood up and began to clap and sing a traditional melody with an accompanying dance.

Now, I am not known as a dance man, but I tell you this: when Mrs Robinseki's hips began to gyrate, I could not fight the urge to join in. I rose from the sofa, my trembling hands clutching the biscuit tin in front of me to cover my awkwardness, and caught the rhythm of her moves.

It was with much guilt that I left that meeting – feelings of ecstasy still flowing through my legs while I passed the drawing room where the deceased Mr Robinseki was lying in a casket. The Hobnobs had been reduced to a sticky soup of molten chocolate, oatmeal, and dead flies, so I left them in the mansion courtyard next to a statue of Dame Shirley Bassey – a favourite singer of Mrs Robinseki from the old days.

*

"How does this sound?" I asked her the next day as I paced my living room, reading a draft letter: "'I am Mr Benjamin Mbibi-yaya, personal attorney of the late Mr Thomas Robinseki, Finance Minister of Nigeria, of blessed memory, may his soul rest in peace. I have a mutually benefiting business proposal for a trustworthy foreign partner ...'"

Mrs Robinseki watched me with her gorgeous brown eyes. When I had finished, and stood awaiting her verdict, she smiled and said, "You write like an angel."

My knees weakened, forcing me to grab the back of a chair for support before allowing myself to slump into it.

She mulled over our plan. "Do you have anyone in mind?"

"I have a list of people," I said. I thought it best not tell her it had come from a Facebook page devoted to dogs with exceptional singing and dancing potential.

"And the partner would get $10 million?"

FLIES, DAMNED FLIES, AND STACKED BISCUITS

I nodded. "For their trouble, and in compensation for the small administrative fee of $100,000 they'd need to provide upfront to release the funds."

"Excellent!" Mrs Robinseki grinned. Then she approached me. "Such a clever boy." She swept a hand through my hair, causing not just my hopes to rise. "You are sweating, Benjamin. It is a lucky sign."

*

A few days later, when she Skyped to ask how it was going, I had to admit I hadn't received a single response to my e-mails, even though I had sent over 100.

It was the same story when she contacted me a week – and another 100 e-mails – later. I did not tell her about the seven abusive replies I had received, nor about the two messages threatening me with the police. There is no understanding some people. Here was the opportunity of a lifetime to earn a large sum of money for hardly any effort, and all they could do was insult and threaten me!

Worse, Mrs Robinseki seemed to be losing faith in me. So, I upped my rate of mailing until, at last, a promising response came back. I Skyped Mrs Robinseki immediately, and she took me to an expensive cafe to celebrate. I cannot tell you the joy I felt.

The happiness lasted but six days. The cheque for $100,000 duly arrived from Mr Michael Mouse of Penge, London, and I took it to the bank – only to learn a day later that it had bounced, and I would be liable for bank charges. The shock of this was great. How can anyone perform such a brazen act of dishonesty? Unbelievable. Really, you cannot trust people these days. It is a very, very sad state of affairs.

And so, unhappily, that is how things stand at present. The $600 million is still in the bank and out of reach, and

Mrs Robinseki does not return my calls. I am beginning to lose hope.

But, my dear Reader, maybe you can help. If you are an honest person, and interested in a business proposition that would make you very rich, please contact me, Mr Benjamin Mbibi-yaya, on b.mbibiyaya@gmail.com. This is real. It is not Science Fiction.

Changes

"Ah, Sheila. I'm so glad you came." Professor von Craniken beckoned me into his laboratory. "I think you'll find this interesting."

I rather doubt it, Prof, was my unvoiced response. Any mention of Science and suddenly I'm remembering a pressing engagement elsewhere.

The professor, his eyes wild and his wispy hair waving in all directions, led me past racks of test tubes, piles of electronic equipment and stacks of papers. He stopped at what looked like a space-age Portaloo. The moment he started explaining about fields and fluxes and monopoles, my attention drifted and something caught my eye. A dumpy, frumpy woman was staring at me from a corner of the lab. Lab assistant, maybe? She had the faintest of sneers on her lips, which I didn't much like the look of. *If that's directed at me, love, the feeling's mutual.*

Looking back at the professor, I noted he had moved on to polarities and singularities and planarities, all explained with flapping arms and hyperactive eyebrows. So, nothing of the remotest interest to man or beast. I found my eyes straying back to the woman. Her face might have been attractive once, but now, with no make-up, and topped with a heap of unkempt hair, the poor thing seemed to have given up on her appearance. Her figure had gone, too – in all directions – and no way was it coming back.

Still that superior sneer bothered me. *Jealous of my looks and cool dress sense, perhaps?* I sneered back.

"And so," the professor was saying, indicating the Portaloo, "I built this Time Machine!"

"Uh-huh," I responded, barely glancing at the device.

"And today I went forward in time." He beamed at me with his crazy, bulging eyes. "As proof, I brought someone back from the future!" He nodded towards the woman in the corner, and her sneer appeared to double in size.

Finally, it began to sink in what he was telling me. And, as it did so, I couldn't help wondering why, of all the people he might have brought back from the future, he had selected this particular, unattractive specimen.

Grinning, von Craniken shuffled towards me and put a hand on my elbow. "Sheila," he said, leading me towards the other woman. "Let me introduce you to ... er ... Sheila. Not a coincidence, ha, ha. No. For, you see, this lady is your future self."

Tree Hugger

The flashing red light on his spaceship control screen made Kroll da Krona's branches sag, and the sap drain from his leafy Afro-like crown. Things did not look good. The ship's hydro pressure was low, and falling. Any second, the Verp-drive would fail – and then they'd be in trouble.

He cast a nervous glance at the ship's other occupant, thankfully still fast asleep, rooted to a nutritious bed of decaying compost. He didn't dare tell her, but what if the alarms went off?

At that precise moment, they did just that. They

jangled and blared while the control room's lights flashed on and off. Kroll stabbed a twiggy digit at a button to kill the sound, but not quickly enough to prevent the other Arborian waking.

"What's happening?" asked Bayla with a start, her silvery grey leaves rustling in panic.

"It's OK, Mum," said Kroll, trying to keep his voice as calm as possible. "Just a minor thing. Nothing to worry about. You go back to sleep."

"How minor is 'minor'?"

"Um, minor-ish."

"The spaceship's broken, isn't it?"

Kroll looked away to avoid his mother's accusing stare. "Er, not completely broken, Mum. Look, the lights still work." He flipped a switch on and off to demonstrate.

Bayla thumped one of her branches down on a table-top. "I knew it!" She thumped the branch again. "I just knew you'd been sold a dud. Didn't I say he was a dodgy dealer? What are we going to do now? You're supposed to be marrying the Holey-C tomorrow."

"Ah, yes," said Kroll, barely able to suppress a triumphant grin; it appeared there was a silver lining to this cloud after all. "Oh dear, it looks like I won't be able to make the wedding. What a shame. Better call the whole thing off."

"Not so fast, Son. You're marrying Holey-C, and that's final."

Kroll gave a deep, deep sigh. "But, Mum …"

"Don't you 'but Mum' me. Holey-C is the cleverest computer in the whole galaxy. It's a massive honour to be chosen to be one of her husbands. She only picks the finest, most upstanding trees with the leafiest crowns and sturdiest trunks."

"You don't think it's a bit weird: a computer marrying a tree?"

"Not when she's as fantastically rich and powerful as she is."

Kroll shrugged his upper branches. "Well, with our Verp-drive blown, we can't possibly get there for tomorrow anyway."

Bayla seethed for a few seconds, but then calmed down and became merely stern. "Have you called the Quadruple-A?"

Kroll shifted uneasily. A couple of loose leaves detached themselves from his upper canopy and fluttered to the soily floor.

"You did renew your membership to Quadruple-A, didn't you?"

"It was on my to-do list, Ma, but, in the rush, I didn't get a chance. Sorry."

"Great. So, we're going to wither and die, adrift in interstellar space."

"Technically, we're not adrift, Mum. We're in the gravitational field of a small planet. Being slowly pulled in. We should be hitting its atmosphere any time now."

Right on cue, the spaceship juddered as it encountered resistance, causing their trunks to bend alarmingly and their thick roots to extend across the deck as they tried to hold on.

"Call the Q-A," cried Bayla, testing her branches for signs of breakages. "Never mind the cost. Your rich wife will surely be happy to pay."

Hiding his reluctance, Kroll turned to the control panel and, with no great show of urgency, sent the message.

Bayla peered out of the nearest porthole at the planet

below. "Your father would never have let this happen," she said with a huff.

"No, Mum."

"Your father would have had a mechanic check every nut and every bolt on this rust-bucket before he parted with a single *hock* for it."

"Yes, Mum."

"Such a solid Arborian, your father."

"Better hold on, it might get a bit bumpy soon."

"Don't you tell me what to do. Your father never told me what to do."

In his mind, Kroll counted to ten. "I'm merely offering advice, Mother dear. It's to stop you getting any fractures when we touch down. You know how brittle your branches are."

With a snort, she wrapped herself, root and branch, around the solid framework of the spaceship. "I don't much like the look of that planet." She peered down at it again. "Wet-looking. You know how excessive moisture makes my bark peel."

Kroll continued his count, reaching twenty. "When we get down there, we'll stay in the ship and wait for rescue."

"Do you think they play *Blongo*?"

"What? Who?"

"The natives. Down there. *Blongo*."

Kroll rolled the five eyes embedded in his trunk, one after another, but not so that his mother could see. "Possibly ..." he answered. "... not!" he added to himself.

*

As the Arborian spaceship hurtled down through Earth's atmosphere, Kroll studied Earth's *Galactopaedia* page. "Top species: 'humans'. Hmm, quite cute. A bit like the *bab-loons* from ancient times – creatures who spent all day sitting on the branches of our ancestors and defecating. Until we evolved walking, and were able to shake them off."

"*Bab-loons*!" Bayla cried in alarm. "My goodness. We must blast them with our lasers!"

"Er, no, Mum, we don't have any lasers. And Galactic Union regulations make it illegal to shoot any creature smarter than a *maw-lon*. Humans, it says here, are quite clever. They cook with *micro-pingdingers* and eat with *klinkers* and *pronks*."

"Yeah, but who'd ever know if we nixed a few?" said Bayla, one of her branches miming a shooting action. "Your father always said: 'Shoot first, and don't bother asking questions later'. What a guy!"

"I'm afraid times have changed, Ma, and mavericks like Dad are no longer tolerated. That's why he's in prison."

Bayla huffed.

At that moment, the spaceship started shaking wildly. Kroll glanced at his mother. Her old, knotty branches were gripping the support-struts so tightly her bark was beginning to split.

There wasn't much he could do for her. It was every tree for itself. So, he did what any tree would do. He touched his 'lucky' rock, said a little prayer to the Mighty Flanger, and put his mind into an induced state of unconsciousness.

*

When Kroll woke, all was quiet. The spaceship was on the ground and still in one piece and, more to the point, so was he. No branches broken, no great fall of leaves.

His mother was already up and about. She was peering through a window at the scene outside. "What kind of a *schiff-hol* is this?" she asked.

Kroll joined her at the window. The landscape was predominantly green, peppered with what looked to them like prehistoric Arbosaurs. The massive creatures just stood there rooted to the ground, swaying in the breeze, and not saying or doing anything, their crowns a complete, uncultivated mess. In the distance they could see buildings and moving vehicles of some kind. Kroll checked *Galactopaedia Maps*. "Peckham," he said. "We're in a small park in Peckham."

"The sooner we get away from here the better."

Kroll nodded his agreement before reaching again for his lucky rock.

*

Holey-C, the vast supercomputer the size of a planet, drifted through space, performing the sorts of calculations only a planet-sized computer is capable of. It thought computer thoughts and dreamed computer dreams.

Deep, deep within its core, worked its creator, a Drozon called Brian Wiggett, forever tinkering with its circuits and beefing up its processing power and memory storage. For Brian, the Holey-C Project had started as something of a scrapheap challenge over 50 *yens* previously. After a drunken night out with friends, he had thought it would be a hoot to gather the scrap satellite junk orbiting thousands of the Galaxy's planets and use it to build a vast computer-world. Little had he realised that his ramshackle assemblage, riddled with holes, would one day develop its own intelligence. And an odd obsession with tree creatures.

A blinking light caught his eye. He lifted his welding

goggles and put down an oxyacetylene torch to focus on the nearest display screen. It was reporting a distress signal. When he looked closer, his heart sank. The signal was from Kroll da Krona, marooned on a planet called Earth, and unable to make tomorrow's wedding.

"Oh, *bot-ox*," cursed Brian. He knew Holey-C would have received the message too, so he braced himself for the reaction.

A high frequency, tormented wail emanated from one of the computer's loudspeakers on the ceiling above Brian. The wail grew louder and louder until the loudspeaker shook itself from its brackets and crashed to the floor next to his feet, falling mercifully silent. Another speaker, in the adjoining room, took up the call. The wailing turned to groaning, and then the groaning turned to a melancholy moaning. "Oh, oh, my beloved Kroll. My beloved is stranded, far, far away. So very far. My beloved needs me."

Brian rolled his eyes, but nevertheless went next door. "Wiggett!" hissed the loudspeaker. "We must fly to Earth. Immediately. Life or death. Maximum power."

"Do we have to? Really? It is just a tree. The Galaxy is full of them." He reached into a nearby drawer and pulled out a magazine. "Here, take your pick. How about this one?" Brian opened the copy of Tree Monthly at the centre-spread and held it up to a battered camera suspended from a piece of angle-iron. A red light under the camera flicked on and the lens adjusted to focus on the photograph which showed a handsome tree, with a healthy crown of leaves, galloping across a field on a *hosse*.

"Pshaw!" scoffed Holey-C. "I'm not interested in a bimbo like that! Or bamboo, or whatever it is. I want my

Krolly! I want to hug him, and stroke him, and plant him on my surface with all the others."

Brian sighed, sat down at the console, and set a course for Earth.

*

A knock on the spaceship door made Kroll and Bayla freeze. Kroll put a twig to his lips to hush his mother. "If we keep very, very quiet, maybe they'll go away," he whispered.

Bayla crept back across the deck to a far corner of the room where she gathered her branches around her trunk and made like a dumb bush.

The knock repeated.

Hardly daring to breathe, and moving as quietly as he could, Kroll edged towards the door. He peered through the door's window and jumped back in shock when a human face appeared. It was pale, and framed by a mass of ultra-thin, dark threads that sprouted from the top of its bulbous top. He was able to identify its features from the *Galactopaedia* entry he'd been reading: eyes, nose and mouth. The latter was painted red, and its ends were curved upwards.

Kroll gulped. He glanced across at his mother and whispered, "It really *is* like a *bab-loon*."

"Tell it to go away."

Kroll activated the external haler. "Go away and leave us alone," he said, before realizing the creature probably wouldn't understand Arborian. It was no surprise, therefore, that it did not go away. Instead, it raised one of its upper limbs and started waving it.

"It's threatening me, Mum."

"Run it through with the thermal skewer. That's what your father would do."

"We're right out of thermal skewers, Mum. I'll have to suit up and fight it."

"Good plan, Son. For once you're thinking like a true Arborian."

Kroll donned one of the ship's emergency exoskeletal suits. Not, strictly speaking, a fighting suit – it was more for surviving avalanches or shifting heavy boulders -- but it gave his lower branches super strength, and he liked the feeling. He picked up his mother's favourite *Chestnut Five* souvenir tour mug and crushed it with the hydraulically-powered gripper, letting the dust pour to the deck.

In two strides he was back at the door. He fixed his five eyes on the human's two and gestured for the door to open. "Right then, my *bab-loony* friend, let's see how tough you are."

The door had risen no more than a couple of feet when a small, hairy, four-legged creature shot in. As it raced past Kroll's roots the shock caused him to overbalance and the heavy suit did the rest, toppling him backwards to the floor. There he lay, helpless, as the beast weaved through his branches, barking incessantly.

"Mr Tiggles!" came a sharp voice from outside. "Come out of there this minute."

Not understanding a word, Kroll mistook this to be a war cry and found himself trembling. The rustling of his leaves made the Jack Russell even more excited. It bounded over and jumped on and off Kroll's exposed trunk.

"Mum!" cried Kroll. "Help." No matter how hard he struggled, both the suit and the bouncing dog prevented him from righting himself.

Then he noticed that the door had fully opened, and

the human had entered. He stiffened.

The two-legged creature uttered some more sounds before leaning over him.

Kroll shut his eyes. This, surely, was it. Game over. He braced himself.

*

After what seemed half a lifetime, Kroll cracked open an eye. No sign of an axe, or other tree-cutting implement – something to be thankful for. The creature was uttering some sounds. Careful not to make any sudden movements, Kroll stretched out a branch and clicked on *Galactopaedia Translate*.

"Are you OK?" the human was saying. "Can I give you a hand?"

Kroll opened his remaining eyes, relieved the words didn't sound much like a war cry, but puzzled by the offer of a hand when he already had so many of his own branches.

Before he could ponder the question, the human had leaned over him, grabbed a couple of his exoskeleton's struts, and hauled his trunk into an upright position, "Sorry about Mr Tiggles. He's very playful."

Kroll stood, startled, gazing up into the human's face. It was a mighty and statuesque creature, a full two feet taller than him. Impressive, he thought.

"Hi," said the human, her mouth curling upwards even more. She put out a hand. "My name's Susan Swale. I'm an IT technician. You must be from outer space."

Kroll stared at the outstretched hand, still not sure what this hand-offering business was about.

Susan beamed a bright smile. "On Earth we shake hands. It's a sign of friendship." She reached out and grabbed one of Kroll's mechanically-enhanced branches before shaking it up and down. "Ow, ow, ow!" she cried, her cries rising in frequency.

"Sorry," said Kroll, releasing the tongs of his servo-powered grip.

In the corner, Bayla opened her leaves just enough to view the creature and shuddered in horror. "Stay away from the *bab-loon*," she called. "*Fleafs*. It's bound to be infested with *fleafs*!"

Susan massaged her hand as Kroll introduced himself. Then he introduced his mother, and Susan gave her a little wave.

"You two look like *proper* aliens," she said, grinning. "Not like those in *Star Trek*, which are just humans with something glued to their foreheads. I'm like the biggest science fiction nerd ever."

Not having a clue what she was talking about, Kroll made a mental note to *Galactopaedia* her words later. He raised a limb and said, "Just a *tec*." A click of the release switch on his exoskeleton caused it to drop to the floor behind him, narrowly missing the dog and prompting it into a new round of barking.

"Shush, Mr Tiggles," urged Susan.

The dog became quiet as it sniffed Kroll's newly exposed trunk. Then it cocked a leg and sent a stream of warm liquid trickling down his bark and into the compost below.

"Mr Tiggles!" cried Susan, shocked. Then, to Kroll, "I'm so sorry, he gets very excited around … er … trees. I think he's taken a shine to you." She knelt down and attached a lead to Mr Tiggles's collar.

Kroll stared hard at the dog.

"Come," said Susan. "You can stroke him. He loves that." She demonstrated, and Kroll tentatively followed suit. The dog's tail wagged like it was trying to shake it free. Bayla uttered another horrified wail from her corner. "No, no, no."

Then, as both Kroll and Susan were stroking the dog, hand and branch inadvertently touched, and a spark arced between them. Both pulled back. Then Susan slowly reached out and gently ran her fingers through Kroll's foliage – the most intimate of Arborian acts.

Kroll swallowed.

They gazed at one another for a few seconds before Bayla broke the silence. "The Holey-C ain't going to like this. No, siree. She's not going to like this one bit."

"The Holey-C? Who's that? Girlfriend?" Susan probed.

"Oh, no one. No one important anyway."

A sarcastic laugh came from a corner of the room. "No one important?" shrieked Bayla.

Kroll quickly changed the subject. "Would you like me to show you around the ship?"

"You betcha. This is a dream come true."

"No one important?" Bayla was still exclaiming.

Kroll led the way into the next room, describing the ship's many neat features and various advanced sensory interfaces. He omitted to mention that most of the features weren't working at the moment, although he did flip a switch on and off a few times to show how well the lights functioned. Susan gazed in star-struck awe at everything. All the while, Kroll's mother tutted in the background, and the dog, which was following them, wagged its tail.

"I'd take you for a spin," said Kroll at the end of the tour, "but the Verp-drive has conked out. We've sent a distress signal, just waiting for someone to come and rescue us."

"How long will that take?"

Kroll shrugged. "Dunno. Maybe within the next 10 sentils."

Susan nodded as though knowing what that meant. "Would you like to wait at my place? I can show you my science fiction collection."

Kroll hesitated.

Susan pointed through one of the windows. "It's just the other side of the park. You can see it from here."

"I'd love to." He turned to Bayla. "Mum, do you want to come with us?"

Bayla's face had a look of disgust on it. She flicked her leaves one way and then the other, as though making secret non-verbal signals.

"Well?"

"I'm not going anywhere. Not with a bunch of *babloons* on the loose."

*

Outside in the park, the light was starting to fade as the day drew to a close. Here and there, the few park lights that hadn't been vandalized, switched on. The clouds rolled in, and they felt the first few drops of rain.

Susan threw a stick for Mr Tiggles to chase before noticing the rain. "We'd better take cover," she said. "They forecast heavy showers."

Kroll looked amused by the idea. "I'm a tree," he pointed out.

"Let's take cover anyway." She grabbed Kroll by a branch and broke into a run, pulling him with her. Kroll stretched his roots and ran like he'd never run before.

Had anyone been watching at that moment, they would have witnessed a surreal sight – a young woman and a dwarf tree with a perfectly manicured pom-pom, running hand-in-branch across Peckham Park. But the only observer of this First Contact between human and ET was Mr Tiggles. And, he, being a dog, was too dumb to spot anything out of the ordinary.

As the rain turned into a torrential downpour, Susan yelled, "There. Over there. Head for those trees."

A final mad sprint and they tumbled, laughing and giggling, under the protective canopy of a large horse chestnut tree.

"Wow, look at me, sheltering under a prehistoric Arbosaur. That's, like, crazee!" said Kroll, sitting upright and shaking his leaves dry. Mr Tiggles joined in, spraying water everywhere.

"Stop it, you two," laughed Susan, "you're making me even wetter." She pulled her wet jumper off over her head, unintentionally exposing a small amount of her smooth trunk before quickly adjusting her T-shirt. Kroll looked away, embarrassed at the wrongness of the feelings he was experiencing.

After a few moments of awkward silence, the rain stopped, and the clear evening sky became visible through the clouds. Kroll pointed upwards. "The beauty of your two moons is nothing to the beauty of your human soul." No sooner had he said it than he was cringing at his own cheesiness.

"Two moons?" said Susan with a laugh. She peered in the direction Kroll was pointing and gasped. "Wow, there *are* two!"

"Their combined magnificence," continued Kroll, "cannot hold a *klankel* to your beauty." He was hoping that his awful chat-up line might actually be working.

But Susan had stood up. "How can there be *two*?"

"Duh. One, two." Kroll pointed to each moon in turn, wondering whether counting was too advanced for humans.

"Earth only has one moon, Kroll, not two."

Kroll's trunk crumpled as if he'd been attacked by a mad lumberjack. An extra moon could mean only one thing: one of those moons was a planet-sized computer.

The Holey-C had come looking for him.

And worse, she had found him.

*

"There they are!"

Kroll heard his mother's distinctive voice before he spotted her emerging from the shadows. She was accompanied by a tall two-legged creature wearing oily overalls, a backpack, and a pair of dangling welding goggles around its neck. As they came closer, Kroll noticed that the two-legged creature was carrying a cardboard box in front of it. There was a hole crudely cut into the front, out of which poked a mechanical eye on a stalk that looked like a bicycle pump. The eye was waving from side to side, gazing up in awe at the massive trees it passed.

They came to a halt in front of Kroll and Susan, who were still lying under the horse chestnut.

"Now you're for it!" hissed Bayla. She turned to introduce the two-legged creature. "This is Brian Wiggett, Holey-C's tekkie. He's brought her with him. In the box."

"Thank you for the introduction, Madam, but I'd like to think I'm rather more than a 'tekkie'. For it was I alone who built the wonderful creation that is Holey-C – the only planet-sized computer in the Galaxy. And, given she is planet-sized, it would be most inaccurate to suggest she is encompassed within this small box. This here is merely a communication device. The computer herself is up there in the sky in all her magnificence."

Bayla, offended, folded her two main boughs and tapped one of her roots on the ground.

The eye-stalk wiggled in an agitated manner and Brian put his finger to his earpiece. He turned to Kroll. "She wants to know why you're canoodling with a *bab-loon* under an Arbosaur when it's supposed to be your special day tomorrow."

Kroll's outer leaves took on a slightly redder shade. "We're not canoodling," he spluttered. "We merely took shelter under this Arbosaur for the duration of a *ren* shower, and a few of my branches seem to have snagged on Susan's clothing. That's all." Kroll cast a guilty look at the cardboard box. "Hi, Holey-C."

But Holey-C didn't respond. Her electronic eye had been distracted by something, and was now peering backwards, around the corner of the box. Kroll followed her gaze: beneath the limbs of the horse chestnut, past the wooden bench, and across the park. There, brightly lit by one of the park's illuminations, and the light of the two moons, was a solitary cherry tree, handsome and pregnant with pink blossom. A light breeze sent a flurry of petals in their direction.

Brian pressed a finger to his earpiece and listened. Then he turned to give Kroll an apologetic look. "Wedding's off, mate," he said. "Sorry." He pulled a spade out from his backpack and headed off in the direction of the cherry blossom tree.

"What wedding?" asked Susan, with a suspicious look.

"I have no idea what they're talking about, Susan.

Must be confusing me with some other Arborian. To some bipeds, we trees all look alike." He uttered a happy sigh, feeling a huge weight had just been lifted from his pollards. Joyous and grinning, he leapt up from the ground, pulling Susan up with him, sending Mr Tiggles into a mad spin. He wanted to hug everyone: Susan, Mr Tiggles, even his mother.

But where was she? He looked around, finally spotting her wandering off in the direction of the bright lights of Peckham High Street. "Where you going, Ma?"

"I think I spotted a *Blongo* Hall."

Kroll gave Susan a pitying glance before calling after his mother, "Later, Mum. Let's do that later. Come with us. Susan's going to show us her science fiction collection."

The Visitor

"Can I help you, sir?" asked the sales assistant, beaming brightly.

Bob gave her a tight smile and shook his head. "I need to speak to the chemist. Personal matter."

The woman glanced across at the white-coated man dispensing tablets. "The pharmacist is busy at the moment."

"That's fine. I'll wait."

"Very well." The woman gave an impish smile before returning to sorting some prescriptions.

Bob waited, fidgeting and shuffling his feet all the while. Every now and then, the sales assistant would look up at him with a little smile, and he would return it with a sheepish version of his own.

Finally, the pharmacist was finished. He beamed with recognition. "How's the ointment working out for you,

THE VISITOR

sir?"

"Fine, fine."

"All clearing up?"

"Yes, sure." Bob hunched his shoulders and beckoned the pharmacist nearer. He lowered his voice. "But I've not come about that. Listen, there's something I need to show you."

The pharmacist's eyebrows rose.

"It's quite important. Well, very important. Can you spare a few minutes?" Bob jerked his head to indicate the door to the street.

Intrigued, the chemist turned to his assistant. "Emily, can you hold the fort for a while? I'm just popping outside with this gentleman."

"No probs, Dilip," she replied.

Outside, Bob led the way down the High Street. "I'll be straight with you. This is something very, very weird. But, if we play our cards right, we could be onto a nice little earner. Well, a nice *big* earner."

Dilip frowned. "I'm not sure ..."

"Don't worry. It's perfectly legit." Bob clapped him on the back. "But if I'm right, we could both be millionaires. Billionaires, even."

"Why me?"

"You'll see,"

Dilip's face became even more concerned. He checked his watch and cast a glance back the way they had come.

Bob was rubbing his hands as he turned a corner into a residential road. "Billionaires," he repeated. Seeing Dilip dragging his feet, he ushered him on urgently. "Come on. This is where I live." He passed through a gate but, instead of heading towards the front door, he made for the garage.

Dilip halted just outside the gate. He wiped his forehead and looked about.

"Trust me. We'll be rich. It's in here." Bob was swinging the garage door upwards. He waved Dilip towards him, an insistent look on his face.

With halting steps, the pharmacist approached the garage. Inside, it was dimly lit and filled with the junk of many years. As his eyes adjusted, he noticed a figure sitting on a battered old leather sofa by the far wall. At first, it looked like a wizened old man, perhaps someone's great grandfather. But the more his eyes adjusted, the more the figure came to resemble someone's naked great grandfather. Covered in dark brown fur. With a prehensile tail and large, bulging yellow eyes. Dilip gasped and turned to leave, but Bob had already shut the garage door behind them.

"How do," said the creature in what sounded like a Yorkshire accent.

This made Dilip gasp once more. He looked at Bob, but Bob just grinned and ushered him further into the garage. "Let me introduce you guys." He indicated the wizened creature on the couch. "This is Glurt. From Outer Space." The creature bowed its head. "And this is Dilip. From the chemist's around the corner."

"Outer Space?" was all Dilip could say. His mouth had dropped open and he seemed unable to take his eyes off the being before him.

"Show him," Bob urged the alien. "Do that trick you showed me."

"OK, no bother. Now you see me." The alien disappeared. "Now you don't."

"See?" said Bob, beaming. "Nice trick."

The alien reappeared.

THE VISITOR

"How …?" asked Dilip.

Glurt's bulging yellow eyes sparkled. "You see, I'm not actually here. I'm just a projection from my starship up in orbit. I can switch it off and on again." He did so, two more times.

Dilip was shaking his head in disbelief.

"Fortunately, he speaks English." Bob was almost bouncing with excitement.

The alien appeared to chuckle. "I speak all your planet's languages, including dolphin, whale and a smattering of goat."

Bob gave an exaggerated laugh. "Anyway, here's the scientist you wanted to speak to, Glurt," he said. "He's a chemist."

"Pharmacist," corrected Dilip.

"Grand," said the alien. "A scientist. Just the man."

Suddenly, Dilip looked like a cornered rabbit. "I'm not a research scientist, you know."

"Whatever," said Bob, patting him on the shoulder. "You're the only scientist I know. Chemist, physicist, pharmacist. It's all the same, isn't it?"

"Fine by me, too," said Glurt. "Reet, park yer backside and let's get started. You know some basic science, right?"

Dilip nodded, although not in a particularly convincing manner. Still a little shell-shocked, he seated himself on an old breakfast stool, while Bob sat down on a tea chest.

"Anyways," started Glurt. "I was on my way to t'Galactic High Council and thought I'd pop by. See how things are going down here, like." He frowned. "And it doesn't look good, my friends. Not good at all. Scans show the global temperature rising at what will soon be an unstoppable, runaway rate. Catastrophe awaits you. Dramatic climate events, mass starvations, wars leading to nuclear conflict – much faster than you fellas realize. Your species will soon be extinct."

Dilip and Bob exchanged grim glances.

"Cheer up. It's not the end of the world – yet," Glurt sniggered at his own joke. "I'm here to help. Shouldn't really. We're not supposed to interfere with primitive lifeforms, but ... well ... I'm kind of fond of this place and you guys." He leaned forward and, in a hushed whisper, added, "I've helped out before, you know. Couldn't resist. Came down, dropped the odd hint or two. I expect the people I spoke to became rich and famous and are now household names." He leaned back with what looked like a satisfied grin.

Dilip glanced at Bob who merely winked back and tapped the side of his nose.

"Elvira Baumgartner," said Glurt in a dreamy manner, as though at a fond memory.

"I beg your pardon?" asked Dilip.

"I expect she's famous."

"No," said Bob and Dilip together.

"Inventor of time travel."

The two men shook their heads.

"Oh," said Glurt, disappointed. "You mean you don't have time travel?"

Again they shook their heads.

Glurt frowned. "I wonder what happened there. Maybe Elvira went back in time and hasn't returned yet." He shrugged. "How about Paul Barnsley. You've surely heard of him."

Bob grinned. "Of course! Played for Newcastle and Liverpool."

THE VISITOR

Dilip was wagging a finger at him. "You're thinking of Peter Beardsley."

"Ah, you're right."

Glurt looked thoroughly put out. "Paul Barnsley. 'Inventor' of faster-than-light travel?"

The two men looked blank.

"You don't have faster than light travel?"

"Nope."

"Hmm, what could have happened to Paul? Never mind. We have a more pressing problem to deal with here: preventing world catastrophe." He sat forward. "You see, there's a very simple solution to all your energy problems. I'm amazed you guys haven't discovered it already. It's all to do with the properties of the hydrogen atom. You know about the hydrogen atom, don't you?"

Dilip nodded his head, but Bob rose. "Woah, you lost me at 'hydrogen', buddy. Science – never my strong point. I'll go make a cup of tea. You guys want a cuppa?"

"Please," said Dilip, who seemed to have calmed down a bit. "Milk, no sugar."

"Not for me," said Glurt. "I can't drink …"

"You sure?"

"… on account of being a projection."

"Ah, gotcha." Bob laughed and left the garage. He was grinning like a Cheshire cat and whistling a happy tune as he made his way to the kitchen.

"You sound cheerful," said Glenda, coming to see what the noise was about.

Bob grabbed her gaily around the waist and danced her round the kitchen. "We are going to be rich and famous, my love. Mark my words. Can't tell you the details just yet; it's all a bit hush-hush. But we will be richer and more famous than in even your wildest dreams."

"Where have I heard that before?"

"Sure-fire winner this time, dear. Plus we'll be saving Mankind into the bargain. That's going to be worth a knighthood, at the very least. And a Nobel Prize. Possibly two." He gave her a quick peck on the cheek. She threw him a sceptical look and left him to it.

Bob was still beaming as he returned to the garage with the two mugs of tea. The alien was explaining something, waving his hands and flicking his tail, while Dilip sat nodding his head. It sounded fiendishly complicated to Bob. He handed Dilip one of the mugs and sat down to sip his own.

After about half an hour, Glurt concluded with, "And that's all there is to it! Simple. It will solve all your problems and save your planet."

Dilip took a deep breath. "Wow," he said. His face was red and his eyes sparkled like those of someone who had just been converted to a new religion. He smiled at Bob and gave him a thumbs-up. Then he turned to Glurt and thanked him profusely. He tried shaking the alien's hand, but his hand merely passed through the projection.

"Think nothing of it," said Glurt. "Just trying to help out. I can't stand by and see a semi-intelligent species wipe itself out." He sighed. "Gotta be going now, or I'll be late for the meeting. Good luck. Bye."

And he vanished.

For a long time, Bob and Dilip stared at the spot he had just vacated, each lost in their own thoughts.

Then Bob broke the silence. "See. Told you it would be worth your while. Right. First things first. We've got to patent those ideas. Then we start looking to sell them to some massive company that can implement them. And then, wealth and fame await us! We'll split everything 50-50."

But Dilip's expression had grown concerned and he seemed to be staring into the distance.

"What's wrong?" asked Bob. "You don't like the split? We can make it 60-40 to you, if you prefer. I'm fine with that."

"No, it's not that," said Dilip, stroking his chin and frowning.

"What is it, then? We're saving Mankind here."

"Hmm."

"What's wrong?"

"Well, do you remember the first time someone showed you how to tie a shoelace when you were a kid?"

Bob looked baffled. "Yeah?"

"It seemed so easy, so straightforward. Each step was simple on its own …"

"Go on."

"But when you tried it yourself you realised you hadn't grasped it at all, and couldn't even remember the first step."

"Uh-huh."

"It's like that for me now. I don't think I got anything of what he told me."

Bob's eyes widened. "But you were nodding your head. I saw you."

"Sure. Nodding seemed the polite thing to do. Glurt was obviously trying so hard to make the explanation easy for me."

"Didn't you take notes?"

"No."

"Or record the conversation on your phone?"

"Didn't think of that." Dilip sighed. "I wonder if it

was the same for Elvira Baumgartner and Paul Barnsley. He spoke so fast. And there was a lot to take in. And his Yorkshire accent made some bits really hard to understand."

They stared at each other in silence for a minute. Then Bob jumped up and rummaged around in an old drawer before pulling out a pile of scrap paper.

"Quickly, tell me everything you remember. I'll write it all down."

Dilip stood up and took a few thoughtful paces before settling down on the leather sofa with his hands clasped behind his head and his gaze fixed firmly on the garage ceiling.

"I remember there was a lot of talk about hydrogen. Write that down – hydrogen."

"OK. Got that. Item 1."

"Then Glurt talked about saving the planet."

"Right. Save the Planet. I'll put that at the end of the list."

"And he kept banging on about how important it is to act quickly before it's too late. Which unnerved me a bit. After that it was a bit hard to concentrate – and that's when I started nodding."

"So what should I put down between 'hydrogen' and 'Save the Planet'?"

Dilip returned his gaze to the ceiling. Then he sat forward. "Quark field! I remember him mentioning a quark field."

Bob punched the air and scribbled it down. "Great. This is great. Keep going."

"Quantum number. Oscillating column. Dipolar excitation energy."

"Fantastic." Bob was beaming broadly as he wrote the

words down.

"Monochromatic laser induction."

Bob was bouncing with excitement. "We're on a roll. Not sure I got the spelling right, but it doesn't matter. What else?"

Dilip's face dropped and he grimaced. He scratched his head and looked this way and that. "Er, I think that's it."

"Come on. There's got to be more. Think, man, think!"

Dilip thought. For five minutes he sat wracking his brain. Eventually, he said, "Nope, that's all."

Bob slumped. "That's not much, really. From a half-hour explanation."

"Don't lose heart." Dilip gave him a consoling pat on his writing arm. "Hand me the list."

Bob looked hopeful. But, after staring at it for a full minute, Dilip merely handed it back, shaking his head all the while. "Nope, I've got nothing more. Just random words. Nothing to connect them."

"So," concluded Bob, "this won't make us rich and famous."

Dilip shook his head again. "And it won't save Mankind, either."

"Oh, yeah. I'd forgotten about that. I guess we're all doomed then."

The Jinx

Roland McLintock was experiencing what was, for him, a rare sense of optimism. Maybe today his luck would change.

It had to.

For today was the Big Match: the West Scotland 4th Division relegation play-off between his team, Dumbarnock FC, and Tiree Old Men. The losers would be relegated and, with no lower football league to drop into, would have no one to play against next season. It was a massive, must-win game.

As he made his way to his usual seat, Roland looked at the pitch to check out the opposition. They were a bedraggled-looking mob, standing in what could only be described as an unorthodox football formation; something like 2-1-1-3-1-2. Some were wheezing, others crouched with hands on knees, seemingly already exhausted from the warm-up, while the left back was having some problem with his underwear that required constant

THE JINX

attention.

Surely, we can beat this lot, thought Roland.

Tiree Old Men were aptly named; their average age seemed to be around seventy. An outbreak of leprosy on their remote Scottish island had decimated the team. Indeed, according to the matchday programme, they had been forced to name a sheepdog called Patch as a substitute. Roland spotted the dog lying in front of the substitutes' bench. It was a mangy creature, panting hard, with a string of drool dripping from its long tongue. It looked almost as old as its teammates, yet there was a confidence in the dog's eyes that unnerved Roland.

He shuffled along row 13 to seat 13, and sat down next to his only friend in Dumbarnock, Dr Kirk Wu.

"Hurree up! They about to kick off," called Dr Wu in a loud whisper. Dr Wu was a rather short and impatient man, a Chinese Scot, and the only mobile dentist in the west of Scotland.

"Sorry I'm late, Dr Wu. I left my car window open last night, and this morning a swarm of killer bees had taken up residence. So, I had to walk."

Dr Wu rolled his eyes. He was used to the outrageously unlikely things that were always happening to his friend. After all, Roland's name was in the *Guinness Book of Records* as the "world's unluckiest person", albeit misspelt as Ronald McTinLock. He'd received the title after losing 130 consecutive coin tosses. He could have gone on longer but, on the 131st throw, the official Guinness tosser had flipped the coin too high. It had bounced off a roof truss, pinged off a metal light-fitting and dropped into a fuse box where it had wedged between the contacts. The resultant short-circuit had caused an explosion that had started the fire that had burnt the Dumbarnock Community Hall to the ground.

The kick off was being delayed while one of the Tiree Old Men lay on the pitch receiving defibrillator treatment. Meanwhile, the crowd was becoming restless, not so much at the delay, but at Roland's arrival, which had drained all pre-match confidence like bathwater down a plughole. In no time, the fans' negativity transmitted itself to the Dumbarnock players on the pitch and, one by one, they looked up to where they knew Roland would be sitting and their shoulders slumped. Dumbarnock's beleaguered manager, Murray McDougal, turned to give a hard stare at the man he blamed for jinxing his team.

"Up the 'Nockers," Roland mouthed, limply waving a yellow and black scarf at Murray. The manager mouthed back a stream of expletives the like of which had seldom been heard west of Glasgow's St Margo's Convent.

"Me think, Mullay not happy see you," said Dr Wu, offering Roland his tub of popcorn.

"It'll be fine. Those Tiree guys can barely stand. Look at that bloke …" Roland jabbed a finger in the direction of the Tiree goalie and laughed, "… he's wearing a neck-brace. There's no way we can possibly lose to this bunch. Can we?"

Dr Wu scrutinized Roland for a moment but said nothing.

High in the sky, the black cloud that seemed to follow Roland around wherever he went, settled itself into place above the football ground and opened up. As the rain teemed down, it became apparent why no one else would sit in seat 13, row 13. The corrugated iron roof that covered the stand had one hole in it: directly above seat 13, row 13. Roland flipped up his hood against the large drips of rain splashing on his head. He'd tried nearby seats before, but each time a gentle breeze had sprung up to ensure the droplets reached his pate and left him soaked wherever he sat.

Roland's presence at the ground wasn't wholly unwelcome. For a start, the Tiree players were grateful he was there as his presence offered them real hope. Then there was their sole travelling supporter, an old fisherman from Tiree, still in the early stages of leprosy but well enough to make the long trawler trip to see his father play. Finally, there was a mysterious figure lurking behind the east end goal, in the shadow of Dumbarnock's gasometer. The figure, dressed in a black robe and hood, was ignoring the lack of action on the pitch, and instead focusing all his attention in Roland's direction. Roland took no notice, assuming him to be a talent scout from Paisley, on a wasted journey, given there was no talent worth scouting, certainly not on the pitch.

At last, the medical team had managed to get the ailing Tiree man back onto his feet and had returned to the dug-out, leaving him looking bewildered and tottering slightly. The match was ready to start.

No sooner had the whistle blown than the first goal was scored, in a record time of 5.8 seconds. Receiving the ball from the kick-off, Dumbarnock's star player had spotted Tiree's neck-braced goalkeeper off his line and resolved to test him at the earliest opportunity. He hoofed a thunderous shot goalwards from just inside his own half. Unfortunately, he failed to hoist it high enough to clear the Tiree player just 10 yards in front of him and the ball smacked into the man's forehead. The impact rendered Doddy Campbell, Tiree's lighthouse keeper, instantly unconscious. But worse than that, the resulting ricochet sailed half the length of the pitch in the opposite direction, bounced over the head of the hapless Dumbarnock goalkeeper and up into the roof of the net. One-nil to Tiree Old Men.

The tired groan from the crowd was to be the first of many. With Doddy stretchered off, Tiree brought on their canine substitute and, even though Patch was untrained and untested on a football pitch, he turned out to have a natural flair for the game few could have predicted.

"Come-bye, Patch!" yelled Tiree's captain, Jock Maddock, a shepherd with over 50 years' experience. He inserted two fingers into his mouth and gave a series of whistles. The dog responded with a long clockwise run up the left wing. "Steady, boy." Patch slowed and lowered his body, eye on the ball. "Time-now," the captain yelled and accompanied the command with a piercing whistle. The dog pounced, steering the bald, spherical, legless sheep safely into its paddock. Two-nil.

From that moment on, the game was over; the Dumbarnock players were mere spectators as Patch dribbled, scrabbled, jumped and nosed the ball into the net over and over again. Eighteen goals later the referee blew the final whistle to end the home crowd's misery.

The hooded figure behind the east end goal nodded, as though acknowledging some profound truth, and then was gone.

Every eye in the home stand turned an accusatory glare in Roland's direction.

Roland swallowed hard. "It was hardly my fault," he mumbled to no one in particular. It wasn't as if he'd bred and trained the match-winning mutt himself. "We were a bit unlucky there," he said to Dr Wu at his side.

"Sure thing, it bloody unlucky. No way should dog

play. No way." Dr Wu stood up and ushered Roland to leave as quickly as possible. "Come, we go now. Before crowd turn ugwee."

The fans' attention was pulled away from Roland and drawn to the pitch where chairs were being brought on for the victorious Tiree players to have a nice sit down in celebration. Reviving cups of tea followed soon after. Patch weaved in and out of the chair legs, collecting well-earned pats and titbits. The home fans watched on in stunned silence, taking in the dreadful consequence of the defeat. No more football for Dumbarnock FC. Ever.

As Roland and Dr Wu made their way through the exit turnstile, the crowd were beginning to recover from the shock and looking for someone to blame. A small group of unruly supporters spotted Roland leaving the ground and began waving their arms around. "Don't let him get away, lads," one of them shouted.

*

From a cloaked spaceship, beyond the orbit of the Moon, the Espadrips were monitoring Roland's movements. They had crossed the Galaxy in search of the legendary Jinx – a being whose superpowers they believed could save them.

"That was unbelievable!" said Colin the Considerate, a pimple-faced Espadrip, turning his bulbous head from his monitor to his queen, Madam Vorg the Honourable. "Did you see that, your Highness? How the dog ran rings round them?"

"Wondrous," replied Madam Vorg. "Such an improbable outcome could only be the work of The Jinx."

Colin turned back to his monitor, now showing an angry gang of Dumbarnock supporters squeezing through the turnstiles and charging towards Roland with obvious malevolence. "Majesty, I wonder if now might be a good time to step in and save him."

"Splendid idea, Colin. You're such a clever boy. Could you please give our surface agent a tinkle and arrange an extraction? Ask nicely. And remember, Colin, The Jinx must believe that we are an evil and violent race, not the wimps we really are. Otherwise our plan will fail."

"Of course." Colin unhooked the communicator from his utility belt, tapped the display and held it to his pointed ear. "Hello, is that Ivor the Caring?" There was a squeaky response that only Colin could hear properly.

"You mustn't call him that!" hissed the queen. "It'll give the game away. His undercover name is Ivor the Vicious. Don't forget."

Colin nodded. "Sorry to bother you, Ivor the Vicious, but Madam Vorg the Child-Slayer here – that's what we have to call her – was rather hoping you could rescue The Jinx before he gets battered to death. She did say 'please'."

Madam Vorg nodded at that. "Ask him to do it quickly, please." The mob on the screen appeared to be moving in for the kill.

Colin put a finger in his other ear so that Vorg's raised voice didn't drown out Ivor's reply. "Oh, that's excellent news, Ivor. You're ready to swoop, you say?" Colin gave a smile and a nod to the crew who were all trying to listen in. "And you'll be with us very soon? Well that's marvellous. Simply terrific."

Vorg tapped Colin's elbow and mimed the most vicious face she could muster and pawed the air as if she had talons.

"Hold on a minute, Ivor. Madam Vorg the Child-Slayer is trying to tell me something." Colin tapped the communicator to put Ivor on hold. A tune, remarkably similar to the A-Team theme music, played.

"Don't forget the bit about pretending to be a vile monster," said Vorg, waggling a finger at Colin's communicator, urging him to get on with it.

Colin lifted the device and killed the music. "Hello, Ivor the Vicious. Are you still there?" He nodded to his audience to confirm that Ivor was still on the other end. "Great. Listen, Madam Vorg is very keen that you make out like you're a very mean bad guy."

The squeaking increased in volume on the other end of the communicator and Colin wandered over to a quiet corner of the spaceship.

"Yes, yes, everyone knows you're not like that. We've all heard of your voluntary work with the baby *golfins* at the Watery Sanctuary. But, remember your mission! The Jinx must think that we Espadrips are the bad guys and our evil enemy – the Sirloins – are the goodies."

(More squeaking)

"I know, I know, it's very confusing. Don't worry too much about the details, just act as badly as you can, there's a good chap."

(Squeak)

"Okay ... bye ... yep ... see you later ... bye ... bye ... bye." Colin clipped his communicator back on his utility belt and turned to the crew. "He says he'll do his best."

*

By the mobile dentist van, Dr Wu was frantically patting his pockets in search for the keys as the angry mob advanced.

"Quick as you can," urged Roland, casting an anxious glance behind him.

"Found them!" Dr Wu gave the keys a quick wave before pressing the unlock button on the fob.

Just in time, the two scrambled into the front seats of the van, slamming and locking the doors behind them. What was left of the angry mob, namely six surly youths, surrounded the van. The rest had decided that Dumbarton FC weren't actually worth fighting about, and so had dispersed into the rundown streets around the ground.

A loud thump shook the van as the hefty right boot of one of the six connected with Roland's door. The others put on their most menacing expressions.

"Come oot, come oot, or I'll blow yer hoose doon," said the leading thug, brandishing the only weapon he'd been able to find on his journey across the car park – a traffic cone.

Roland cracked his window half an inch and pressed his mouth to the gap. "If it's money you're after, I'm afraid we don't have much. But here's a quid." He pushed a pound coin through the gap in the window. It fell to the tarmac, bounced a couple of times and then rolled through a gully grating from which could be heard a faint Plop!

"It's nay yer money we're after, yer wee quivering jellyfish. Yer've cursed the 'Nockers with yer bad luck and we're doon and oot of the league. So now it's payback time!"

The other hooligans edged closer. They, too, had an assortment of improvised weapons: a hubcap, an empty plastic coffee cup, a bent bicycle wheel, and a small tree.

"Stop, please!" boomed a voice that halted the thugs in their tracks. It came from the same hooded figure Roland had previously spotted at the ground. "I am Ivor the Viscous and I ask ... nay ... *command* you to put down your weapons."

Up this close, Roland could see the mysterious figure was a lot taller than the thugs and this, in itself, was enough to make some of them drop their makeshift armaments. Furthermore, on its face the figure had what appeared to be a Halloween Frankenstein monster mask made of cheap plastic, bringing to mind the serial killers of horror movies. More weapons hit the ground.

But as the figure stepped forward, the lad armed with the traffic cone, who had not dropped his weapon, gave it a mighty swing, first into Ivor's midriff, causing the Espadrip to buckle over, and then in an uppercut motion into the alien's face, causing him to collapse to the ground like a sack of potatoes. He lay there, holding his groin and whimpering. The elastic band holding the Frankenstein mask had snapped, revealing a soft, angelic face – more like a choirboy's than that of a serial killer or righteous avenger.

The thugs now turned back to the dentist van, and once more advanced on it with renewed malice. Roland and Dr Wu pressed themselves back in their seats, quivering. For a moment, they had held out hope of rescue by their would-be saviour. Now, all hope seemed lost.

Just then, a shopping trolley with a full load of shopping, and toddler in a child-seat, rattled past Roland's side-window. Behind it was a hefty woman with a furious expression on her face. She pushed the trolley faster and faster, heading directly at the principal thug. The hooligan didn't stand a chance, and the trolley rammed into his legs.

"Ooch, mum!" he cried. "That hurt."

"I'll give yer something to 'ooch' about when I get yer

home, Kenneth McCrae," boomed the woman, her gravelly voice sounding more male than female. She grabbed the lad's earlobe in a twisting grip with one hand while helping the crumpled Ivor to his feet with the other. "I'm so sorry, mister. I hope my doaty bampot of a son has nay damaged yer doonstairs department." Mrs McCrae dipped her head to indicate his lower region.

Then she set off with shopping trolley and son in tow. The other thugs had melted away, only too aware of Ken's mum's foul tempers and their consequences.

Ivor grunted and staggered over to the van, propping himself against the bonnet, still bent over from his injury.

Roland and Dr Wu climbed out, with Roland placing a consoling hand on Ivor's back. "Are you alright, mate? Thanks for trying to help us back there. Much appreciated, pal."

Dr Wu nodded. "You velly kind man."

Ivor grabbed the broken Frankenstein mask from where it was dangling on his chest and held it over his face. He stood bolt upright, realizing that things weren't going to plan. "You are mistaken. Ivor the Viscous does not help anyone. Ivor the Viscous is not a very kind man. Ivor the Viscous is known throughout the Galaxy as a torturer and a tyrant." His legs wobbled a bit as he finished speaking.

"Of course, you are," said Roland, making a secret gesture to Dr Wu to indicate a possible drink problem. "Anyway, I'm Roland McLintock ..."

Ivor took a horrified step back. "But ...," he started. "You mean you are not Ronald McTinLock??"

Roland shook his head. "No, that was a misprint in the *Guinness Book of Records*."

"But you *are* the world's unluckiest person,"

"Yes, absolutely."

"Phew, that's a relief."

Roland wasn't sure what to make of Ivor's response. "Anyway, this is Dr Wu."

Once again, Ivor took a step back, this time in astonishment. "Doctor Who??"

"That right. Dr Wu. Why, you hear about my work somehow?" As if to demonstrate his dentist's artistry, Dr Wu pulled a sonic toothbrush from his top pocket and set the device buzzing, making up and down cleaning motions across his bared teeth.

Another step back, this time in horror. For many years the Espadrips had been monitoring Earth's television broadcasts, and there were two documentaries that had left a lasting impression on Ivor: Kojak and Doctor Who. Consequently, he was all too aware of what the Doctor was capable of with his sonic device.

"I think he might be suffering concussion from that traffic cone injury," suggested Roland.

"We get him in back of van, Dr Wu check him out."

Gently, they guided Ivor towards the rear doors.

"New Tardis?" muttered Ivor, indicating the van.

Dr Wu was nodding. "That's right, I artist. Artist in teeth. You must be famiwiar with my YouTube vids: 'Tooth-busted? Dr Wu ya gonna call?'. And 'Driller Filler'."

Ivor didn't reply, not having the faintest idea what the little man was on about. Instead, he braced himself for experiencing the mind-blowing, trans-dimensional wonder of seeing inside the Tardis.

"Plea to step aboard, Mr Ivor," said Dr Wu, swinging the doors open and stepping aside to let the tall figure through. In the middle of the van was a dental chair, smaller than regular size, to the side of which was a sink. Above, were the various hydraulically operated drills and lights. The remainder of the space was crammed with dental equipment, while the walls were lined with drawers and cupboards containing more dental equipment.

Dr Wu gently pushed Ivor up a step and into the chair. He followed him in, shoving him more and more so that Roland could also enter and force the doors shut. Once they were all in, they could barely move.

Ivor looked about him. "It's smaller on the inside than on the outside!" he said, somewhat wrong-footed by the dimensional anomaly he was experiencing. "Not enough room to swing a *klack*."

"I think Dr Wu needs to have a sort-out very soon," suggested Roland, not happy that his personal space was being severely invaded.

"No problem. Plenty room. You sit, Mr Ivor. Put feet up." Dr Wu pushed Ivor back into the chair and aimed an angle-poise lamp towards his mouth. "I check teeth for free. Say ah."

"Ah?" asked Ivor.

Dr Wu gagged and turned his head away. "My God, it smell like you drink from stinky drain hole. And where all teeth go? None here."

Ivor clamped his mouth shut, suddenly self-conscious about his bad breath. In truth, the Espadrips had long since evolved beyond a need for teeth. They could get their five-a-day from sucking the nutritious ponds and puddles that lay about on their planet. Here on Earth, Ivor had sampled a few of the fluids he'd come across, including a drain, a canal, and the fluids in the troughs in the football ground's toilets. It was possible these were at

THE JINX

least partially responsible for his oral odours.

While Roland and Dr Wu attempted to squeeze themselves as far away as possible from Ivor's bad breath, the alien took the opportunity of tapping a message into his communicator: *Lock onto my coordinates. Three to beam up. Prepare for a surprise!*

*

The spaceship was buzzing. What had Ivor meant? A surprise? What sort of surprise? And why were there three being beamed up and not two? They had not been able to follow events in the car park due to the lack of CCTV cameras to hack into.

Lights began to swirl in the middle of the room as the teleporter re-arranged the atoms of the three being transferred from Earth. The Espadrip crew hastily put on the horror-masks Ivor had bought earlier at Morrisons supermarket and beamed up to them. By far the scariest was the Donny Osmond mask, with its perfect white teeth stretched across the face. They had given it to Colin the Considerate.

Suddenly, the coalescing shapes solidified and there was a loud thump – the sound of Ivor falling to the floor, there no longer being a dentist's chair to hold him up. The Espadrips gasped with concern, and two of them ran to help him.

"I'm fine, I'm fine," said Ivor springing to his feet. "Don't worry about me."

Roland and Dr Wu clung to each other in terror as they found themselves surrounded by a collection of terrifying, and some not-so-terrifying, masks. How had they ended up on a spaceship in the middle of a Halloween party?

Vorg stepped forward, hidden behind a Mr Bean mask,

and tried to make her voice as low and terrifying as she could. "Ha! You may very well tremble with terror, Jinx ... and the other one." She stared hard at Dr Wu for a full two seconds before Ivor gave a discreet cough and corrected her. She swung to Roland and stared at him instead. "Ah, *you* are The Jinx. Ronald McTinLock, I presume!"

"Roland," said Roland in a quiet squeak, his voice quivering. "McLintock."

Vorg veered to stare at Ivor. "What is the meaning of this?"

Ivor was shaking his head. "Long story, your Majesty. Bottom line is: this is The Jinx."

The queen seemed to relax before turning back to Roland. "As I was saying, you may well cower, puny Earthling. For we are the Espadrips, known throughout the galaxy as torturers and tyrants. And I am Vorg the Child-Minder!"

"Slayer," put in Colin.

"What?"

"Slayer, your Highness. Child-Slayer."

"Ah, yes, of course. What was I thinking? Thanks."

"No probs."

"So, I am Vorg the Child-Slayer." She indicated Dr Wu. "And who is this foul creature, and what terrible things should we do to it?"

"No, no, Ma'am," put in Ivor. "We mustn't do anything to it. For this is ... well, have a guess."

"Is it Kojak?" asked Colin.

"No, not quite as good as Kojak. But you're close."

"Doctor Who," someone shouted from the back of the spaceship.

"Bingo! How amazing is that?" said Ivor.

THE JINX

"Well," said another voice from the back, "Strictly speaking, that's not his-slash-her name. He-slash-she is actually just called the *Doctor*. Doctor Who is just the title of the documentary."

But no one was interested in pedantic hair-splitting when they had a Time Lord onboard. A buzz went through the crew. One went off to his quarters for his autograph book. Others took selfies. Others just stood and gawped.

Vorg had pulled Ivor to one side. "What the *fluff* are you playing at, Ivor. Bringing Doctor Who on board! You know how clever he-slash-she is. If we're not very careful he-slash-she will work out what we're up to and tell The Jinx. And you know what that'll mean ..."

Ivor dropped his eyes to the floor and kicked at imaginary stones. He thought it cruelly unfair to be getting a telling off when he'd been the one who had captured the VIPs. He really felt like arguing back in quite a forceful way. But didn't.

"If we lose the war, Ivor," continued Vorg, "the Sirloins will be cruel masters, of that you can be sure. No more transgalactic jaunts. You'll be lucky to get a job sharpening jousting sticks at the endless Sirloin banquets. Do you want that? Hmm, hmm? Do you?"

Ivor shook his hood. "So unfair," he muttered.

When Vorg turned her attention back to the prisoners she couldn't believe her eyes. The entire crew were cooing at Dr Wu who was demonstrating the correct way to use a sonic toothbrush. There was much gaiety and laughter. Vorg was horrified.

"Incarcerate the prisoners in the torture cage," she ordered, pointing to a toddler's playpen Ivor had bought in IKEA and teleported up. It had been hastily, and somewhat wonkily, assembled in a corner of the spaceship. "They must learn the horror of being captured by the Espadrips. Isn't that right, Ivor?"

"If you say so," said a rather sulky Ivor.

Together with Colin, they gently guided Roland and Dr Wu to their 3-foot high prison and began fiddling with the childproof lock on the gate.

"What do you want from us?" asked Roland.

"Well," said Colin in a whisper, checking that the queen wasn't listening or watching. From his pocket he pulled out a metal bolt and a plastic bracket. "Would you happen to know where these go? They were left over at the end of the assembly. We couldn't work it out from the instructions."

"IKEA?" asked Roland.

"Uh-huh," said Colin.

"Typical," said Roland with a roll of the eyes. "I usually get the kits with some crucial item missing. Now I realize that they must end up in other people's kits as surplus."

"So?" said Colin, tossing the bolt and bracket in his hand.

"I can have them. One never knows when they might come in handy."

"Sure?"

Roland nodded.

Sensing that Vorg was approaching, Colin hastily transferred the items into Roland's hands and tried to look casual. "Would you like some cushions?" he asked the humans.

"Cushions?" asked Dr Wu.

"He's toying with you," interrupted Vorg, giving Colin a hard stare. "Why would a total beast like Colin the

Mutilator provide you with comfy cushions?" The two humans looked at each other and shrugged, still unable to make much sense of their hosts. "No such luxuries for you, we're going to make you stand while we jump through hyperspace to our home world … if that's alright with you?"

Before Roland and Dr Wu could respond, the spaceship jolted, throwing everyone off their feet. The main viewer showed them streaking through a vortex of starlight. After a few seconds, they felt another jolt and the viewer displayed an Earth-like planet ahead. The space all around the planet was filled with red and blue spaceships, zipping about, firing laser bolts at one another, some exploding, others spouting smoke trails and careening towards the planet. It was a horrendous battle, absolute carnage. As they watched they could see that the red spaceships had the upper hand; they were doing most of the firing while the blue spaceships were doing most of the exploding.

"Are you guys at war?" asked Roland as another blue spaceship burst into a fireball close by.

"We're always at war," said Vorg, with a dismissive hand. "We're Espadrips, the most aggressive race in the Galaxy. We've been known to start a war simply because we didn't like the way an alien walked. Who are we fighting here, Colin?"

"Let me see," said Colin pretending to look something up. "Today we're mostly fighting the Sirloins. They're a peace-loving species, never happier than when they're setting prisoners free. They're really big into emancipation. And flowers. They really like flowers." He flashed up a picture of the least aggressive Sirloin he could find. It was a photograph of a young female, not dissimilar to a crocodile, slashing the air with a meat cleaver. "This one's celebrating Harvest Festival, having just returned from cutting a barley crop."

"What you fight them for?" asked Dr Wu.

Colin tapped a keyboard. "They had the audacity to invite us to a peace summit. Imagine that, the Espadrips at a peace summit!" He laughed, and a wave of nervous laughter echoed around the room. Colin glanced at Roland. *Was The Jinx buying it?* The frequency of explosions on screen seemed to be slowing but Colin couldn't be sure.

"Of course," said Vorg. "The only chance you and Doctor Who have of avoiding a horribly painful death is if the Sirloins were to win the war and come to rescue you. But that's not very likely." Vorg turned away from the humans and stood staring up at the screen.

Roland and Dr Wu huddled together and started whispering.

"Oh my God," said Roland. "It looks brutal out there. And in here. We got to hope the Sirloins win."

"It only thing that save us."

"Come on, you Sirloins," chanted Roland under his breath.

"Sirloins, Sirloins," joined in Dr Wu.

Vorg glanced back at them from the corner of her eye and allowed herself a sly smile. The plan seemed to be working. The Jinx was supporting the Sirloins.

And, indeed, the plan was very much working. Outrageous acts of bad luck were starting to hit the Sirloin fleet. It was like a tsunami, with ill-fortune sweeping across the battlefield. One red ship flew into a meteor that just happened to be heading towards the planet. Another suffered a one-in-a-million plasma drive backflow blockage and spontaneously combusted. Several others smashed into one another as a result of, well, sheer bad luck. Soon the viewer was filled with explosions. The course of the war had turned in the Espadrips' favour. The blue ships were winning. The crew grinned under their Halloween masks and secretly made victory punches under their desks.

But Ivor, being an emotive type, couldn't keep his joy bottled for long. The explosion of a major Sirloin command ship was just too much for him. He leapt into the air, shaking both his fists, and screaming, "Suck up the bad luck you Sirloin *fluffers*." Ivor's mask had slipped, both literally and metaphorically.

In an instant, the Espadrip crew were shushing Ivor and jumping on him to calm him down.

There was a hush in the air.

"Oh, I get it," said Dr Wu, the penny dropping. "You using Roland as bad fortune cookie to win war! He think Sirloins the good guys who come rescue us. Velly clever, but you not fool Dr Wu."

Vorg shot an accusing look at Ivor before removing her Mr Bean mask and putting her hands up in the air in surrender. "It's a fair cop, Doctor Who. We should have known we could never outwit a Time Lord."

Roland was blinking and scratching his head, trying to keep up. "What? You mean, you're the goodies and the Sirloins are the baddies? You've been trying to make out you're evil when all the time you're sweet natured extraterrestrials?"

Vorg hung her head in shame. "Sorry. We lied."

All round the ship, the crew were taking off their masks, revealing faces of utter beauty and kindness.

"Terribly sorry for the deception, but it was our only

chance," said Colin as he fiddled with the child lock on the playpen to let them out.

"So," said Roland, feeling suddenly moved. "I want you guys to win!"

A tired groan passed through the ship, one that was familiar to him from the football terraces. The Espadrips hardly dared look back up at the viewer. And, when they did, they saw that, sure enough, the tables were turning once more.

Hope faded fast. The war was turning against them with every exploding blue spaceship. The Jinx had been their one and only hope, and he had almost saved them. Almost.

What could possibly save them now?

Dr Wu, that's who.

The dentist crossed over to Colin, leant down and whispered in his ear. "Tell computer to turn red ships blue and blue ships red on screen." He winked and gave a big smile. "That should do it."

The Worst Man on Mars

A science fiction comedy novel

by Mark Roman & Corben Duke

Preview

1. The Back Seat Kids

08:30, 24th March 2029 – 46, Culpepper Drive, Huddersfield, Yorkshire

Whenever retired science teacher Malcolm Brimble got a 'bad feeling in his water' it was usually a pretty accurate portent of doom. For eight months, in spite of some powerful antibiotics, the feeling had been worsening.

"It's going to be a disaster, Barb," he moaned through the open door of their en suite bathroom.

"They're saying it's looking good," Barbara countered. She was perched on the end of the bed, nursing two freshly made mugs of tea and staring at the TV. The pictures from *Mayflower III*, in orbit above Mars, showed the crew of Britain's first manned mission to the Red Planet high-fiving one another.

Malcolm looked up from his ablutions and caught

sight of the shaven-headed Mission Commander Flint Dugdale. "No, I can't look at him!" He nudged the bathroom door shut to block the offending view of Dugdale spraying the contents of a can of *Stallion* lager into the zero-G atmosphere.

"People change," his wife called through the door.

"Not that one. Not him. Five years I had him. Bottom of the bottom science set."

"Come on, he was a teenager. The mission's so close now; what could possibly go wrong?"

Malcolm cracked the door open. "I think you're forgetting the *Beagle 2* disaster."

"You don't know for sure he was responsible."

Malcolm snorted. Flushing the toilet, he strode out of the bathroom and across the bedroom, pausing only to grab a pair of oily overalls as he took himself off to the garage.

"Don't forget your tea," Barbara shouted after him. Too late, he had already made it downstairs and out the front door.

As she followed her husband with his mug, the TV transmission cut to a commercial break. An astronaut holding a can of lager was perched on the back of a rearing horse, set against the backdrop of a red desert. "*Stallion*, sponsors of *Who Wants to go to Mars,*" said the voiceover. The handsome space-cowboy lifted his visor and took a gulp from his can before thrusting the label towards the camera. "*Stallion* extra-strength lager. Putting *men* on Mars."

In the garage, Barbara found Malcolm in familiar pose: on his back with his Hush-Puppied feet poking out from under the jacked-up MG Midget Mk III sports car that was his pride and joy.

"No use hiding under there, you silly old goat," she said, heading for the business end of the car.

The sound of his wife's approaching flip-flops made Malcolm retreat even further under the protective mass of the vehicle.

She toe-poked his protruding feet. "Listen. You should be proud of yourself. In a few hours' time, one of *your* former pupils will be the first man on Mars. You're a neighbourhood celebrity. I'd milk it if I were you."

"Celebrity, my foot! What happens when the mission goes pear-shaped because Dugdale doesn't know one end of an Ion Drive from the other? What will they say about his science teacher then?"

Barbara sighed. Peering through the open bonnet, past the high tension leads, spark plugs and coolant hoses, she could just make out the oily scowl on his face.

"That school trip to Stevenage in 2002 still haunts me, Barb."

"That was twenty-seven years ago, dear."

"Single-handedly, he destroyed *Beagle 2*. I know it."

Malcolm's mind drifted back to the Airbus, Defence and Space Establishment in Stevenage. The trip to see the construction of the *Beagle 2* Mars lander had seemed to go off smoothly, despite the continual misbehaviour of the thirteen-year-old hoodies in his charge. Back then, before cynicism had set in, Malcolm believed he could turn even the roughest of Grimley Comprehensive's pupils into potential scientists. In particular, he'd regarded Flint Dugdale as something of a Challenge.

On the way back to Huddersfield, the coach had been stopped by the police following a display of mooning from the back seat. A weary-looking Malcolm had stood alongside the police officers as they searched the gang of undersized thugs for drugs, weapons and stolen goods. He barely batted an eyelid at the stash of contraband emerging from their pockets. But there was no hiding his shock at the small collection of space-age locknuts that had been discovered on the young Dugdale, hidden inside a packet of cigarettes tucked into his left sock. Malcolm had been too stunned to say anything, wondering how – and from where – Dugdale had obtained those fixings.

The bad feelings in his water had started soon after and quickly turned into a guilty obsession with the *Beagle 2* mission. He found himself following every update, every newsflash, dreading the worst. And, sure enough, on Christmas Day 2003, contact with the lander had been lost during its descent to Mars.

For years Malcolm had been plagued by nightmares, convinced the young hooligan had removed some vital fixings. And then, one cold January morning in 2015, he awoke to hear his radio alarm announce that the lonely little lander had been spotted on Mars, its petal-like solar panel still closed due to failed, or missing, fixings. Solid evidence, as far as he was concerned, that Dugdale had sabotaged the mission.

And now, by some monstrous twist of fate, that same boy had grown into the man in charge of the spaceship carrying the first group of colonists to Mars. *How could that be?* Malcolm asked himself, not for the first time. *How had they allowed Dugdale to take over after the commander's death?* Malcolm could only think that the brute had somehow bullied his way into command.

Barbara tutted at the distant stare in her husband's eyes and searched for a conveniently flat surface on which to deposit his morning cuppa. Malcolm snapped out of his trance and shook his head as he became aware of her plans. "No, not on there!" he cried.

Too late. She had plonked the mug on top of the car battery, sloshing hot tea over the terminals and causing sparks of electricity to snap, crackle and pop.

Malcolm groaned and laid his head back on the cold, hard concrete as he gazed past the drips to watch his wife flip-flopping her way through the open garage doors and across the lawn. Next door, he could see the lovey-dovey couple making last minute adjustments to their Union Jack bunting. A street party had been scheduled to coincide with the descent to Mars. Malcolm heard the woman call out from the top of a stepladder being steadied by her husband. "Hiya, Babs. Not long now. Malcolm must be so proud to think he taught the first man on Mars!"

"Oh, yes," answered Barbara with a cheerful wave. "Chuffed to bits."

Under the MG Midget Mk III Malcolm grimaced. "First man on Mars? Worst man on Mars, more like!"

2. The King's Peach

20:21 The previous day – Mayflower III

The spaceship's Assembly Room was unusually packed. Mission Commander Flint Dugdale was seated directly in front of the vast TV screen, his greasy hand wrapped around the remote control and his legs spread wide apart. Normally his predilection for darts, snooker and monster-truck racing drove the other personnel away, but right now they were strapped into the cinema-style seating and buzzing with anticipation. The forthcoming programme was a special broadcast, direct from Buckingham Palace. The King himself was to deliver a personal message to the prospective Mars colonists in a programme titled 'A Very British Mission'.

As yet another lager advert commenced, Dugdale shook a fist at the screen and roared in his broad Yorkshire accent, "Gerron wi' it!" He sat, his bloated belly pointing upwards, in the middle of the three front-row seats reserved for crew. On the back of his seat the gold embossed name of 'Mission Commander Chad Lionheart' had been crossed through with a thick marker pen and 'Commandur Dugdale' scrawled in its place. Rows two to four were for the Mars colonists.

Dugdale scratched between his legs with one hand and twirled a fat finger in his ear with the other as crewmember Lieutenant Zak Johnston floated in zero-G into the Assembly Room and made for the front row.

"Aye, aye, Cap'n. Permish to land?" asked Zak, indicating one of the empty seats.

Flint reached under his chair and pulled out a four-pack of *Stallion* extra-strong lager and a jumbo bag of *Cheesy Watnots*. He placed them in the middle of the empty seat Zak was pointing to and snapped the seatbelt into its clip to stop his booty drifting away. "Seat's taken. Chuff off," he growled.

Zak glided around the front, keeping out of range of his commanding officer, and made for the seat on the opposite side. Flint lifted his left leg over the armrest so that his steel toe-capped Doc Marten boot rested across the other empty place.

"No probleemo, Captain Nemo. I'll just float here, shall I?" said Zak.

Dugdale didn't react, so Zak belted himself into one of the empty seats in row 2. Po-faced, tight-lipped Harry Fortune in row 3 now found himself directly behind a bush of free-floating and widely spread dreadlocks. Harry, former stand-up comedian-turned-poet, and the mission's token celebrity, leaned forward and tapped the Medusa-haired lieutenant on the shoulder. "You do realize I can't see a thing because of your hair."

Zak, having turned with a jolt, studied the comedian's thin mouth as he spoke. Although not clinically deaf he had great difficulty hearing much of what went on around him. The ear wax in his auditory canals, together with his earphones, meant that he only registered the very loudest sounds above the steady beat of his personal music directory. He had come to rely on very poor lip-reading skills to understand what was being said. "You want me to sing *Love is in the Air*?" he enquired.

Sitting next to Harry was Miss Emily Leach, daughter of zillionaire nonagenarian mining tycoon Sir Geoffrey Leach. The heavily perfumed middle-aged lady butted in. "Oh, I love that song. Please sing it, Mr Zak!"

"Soz, Lady Em, that song is alien to this mammalian."

"Surely not!" she exclaimed. And then, as if to mete out punishment for such ignorance of a classic, she let rip with a shrill, ear-jarring voice that, to her tin ear, perfectly matched the song in her head. All eyes stared at her. A single backward glare from the commander cut her off in mid-note and made her face redden. Meekly she resumed sipping Earl Grey from a dainty bone china cup. The cup had been 'adapted' for zero-G by the addition of a cheap plastic lid and a vivid-green curly straw. Just as attention was drifting away from her, and her face was returning to its former paleness, she made an embarrassing cup-draining slurp as she sucked up the last dregs, causing her face to flush once more.

Sitting behind Emily was the diminutive Tarquin Brush, only ten years old but already smarter than most of the others. On his knee was 'Mr Snuggles', the robot he had assembled during the journey using wiring and circuits pilfered from around the ship. Tarquin's smiling mother, Delphinia Brush, gave his hand a warm squeeze, proud that her little soldier could have built such a clever robot. Around her shoulders lay the comforting arm of husband Brian Brush, a man rarely far from her side. Both had the nerdy look and spectacles of planetary scientists, which is what they were.

"About friggin' time!" exclaimed Dugdale as the programme's opening titles finally appeared on the screen.

Hardly anyone batted an eyelid at the commander's bad language. Only Delphinia Brush reacted by placing her protective hands over Tarquin's innocent little ears.

On screen, the credits cleared and a panning shot showed what appeared to be a dense rain forest. An elderly gentleman emerged from behind the leaves of a large banana tree wearing a three-piece tweed suit and matching flat cap. Looking somewhat incongruous in the jungle terrain, he sported a brass plant-sprayer in one hand and a fine walking cane in the other. As he stepped out of the tree's shadow he was instantly recognizable by his drooping elephantine ears, anteater nose and deep-set pebble eyes. He removed his hat to reveal a scabrous scalp long since deserted by its mutinous hair.

Commander Dugdale fumbled to unclip his seat belt, all the time gazing reverently up at the screen. He stood to attention.

"Ayeup, you lot. Gerr'off yer fat bums 'n show some respect for t'friggin' King!" Having stood up too aggressively he found himself drifting, head-first, for the ceiling.

"That's just great," mumbled Harry Fortune, "Now I can't see the screen at all."

"Shhh!" beseeched Emily Leach.

Meanwhile, King Charles III was gesturing up at the

huge glass roof above his head. "Simply splendid, isn't it," he was saying, letting the words escape through tightly clenched jaws. "A replica of Decimus Burton's Temperate House. The original is in Kew Gardens, of course, but one had this exact copy built in the grounds of Buckingham Palace." He paused to swat a tiny fly away. "During the past eight months, while *Mayflower III* and its valiant personnel, have been racing towards the Red Planet, I have found myself drawn here more and more. A place to meditate and consider the Universe above. Indeed, I often find my mind drifting across interplanetary space to Mars, and the vast BioDome of Botany Base where, very soon, the first Martian colonists will be standing. I imagine it looking something like this." The king swept his arm in a wide arc to indicate the lush vegetation surrounding him.

"Botany Base," he mused. "Built not by humans, but by a small army of fiendishly clever British robots sent ahead by the National Astronomical Flight Agency. Five years they have toiled, and the result is a tribute to British engineering, British technology and British knowhow."

Dugdale had managed to push himself back down from the ceiling and was stretching the seat strap across his oversized belly. "British know 'ow!" he scoffed.

"Yeah, what could possibly go wrong?" added teenager Gavin from the back row. His sister Tracey sniggered. Brian Brush removed his arm from around his wife's shoulders and held up a shushing finger to the pursed lips of one of his sternest facial expressions. As usual, the teenagers ignored their father.

King Charles cast a solemn frown at the camera. "Our thoughts, of course, go to those three brave souls who have so far perished on this dangerous mission."

Dugdale snorted. "Brave souls, my arse!"

"And yet, one can't help but feel that the successful completion of this two-year mission, there and back, will form a lasting tribute to their memory and their courage."

"Cobblers."

Charles went on to make a feeble joke about Little Green Men, at which most of the colonists, apart from the teenagers, chuckled politely. "And finally, one would like to relay a special message to the colonists themselves. The boffins at NAFA Mission Control tell one that those valiant pioneers, currently in orbit around Mars, will, through some unfathomable wizardry, be watching this broadcast in about six minutes when the transmission reaches their ship." The camera zoomed in on Charles's craggy features. "Good luck, intrepid colonists. Remember, the whole world is watching you. The whole world will see Britain at her best. You are ambassadors for the first nation to land humans on Mars. We are proud of you all."

Plucking a peach from an overhanging branch, the King took a bite out of it and smiled. The edges of the smile twitched at the bitterness of the unripe fruit in his mouth as he turned, parted several tree leaves with his walking cane, and slipped back into the jungle.

Emily wiped a tear from her eye. A few others could be heard making efforts to swallow the lumps in their throats. The teenagers at the back jeered, and the hand-built robot, Mr Snuggles, was trying out some new vocabulary it had just picked up. "Cobblers," it said in a cute chipmunk-like voice. "Friggin' cobblers."

As the credits rolled, Dugdale gave a noisy sniff. "Load of ol' bollocks," he muttered, pointing the remote control at the TV and starting to flip channels, oblivious

THE WORST MAN ON MARS

to the howls of protest that filled the room.

"One hundred and eighty!" boomed a voice from the TV, and Dugdale stopped flipping.

"Magic!" he said, making himself more comfortable in his seat. "Darts."

*

Within seconds the Assembly Room began to empty. First out of their seats were the Faerydaes. Adorabella Faerydae – the mission doctor, holistic healer, spiritual reader and homeopath – floated towards the door. Chiffon, crystal beads and long auburn hair trailed behind her. Husband, Brokk, and their son, Oberon, drifted to her side and like a family of synchronised mer-people they glided over the heads of their colleagues and into the corridor.

Ex-comedian Harry Fortune unclipped his seat belt and launched himself towards the exit, staring miserably down at his Fliptab on which were jotted just a few random rhymes: 'Dugdale – thug fail', 'disaster – plaster', 'doom – gloom'. In his capacity as Poet in Residence he hadn't written a single poem during the entire journey, save for a few feeble love poems for the prettiest passenger, Penny Smith.

Penny Smith, alas, was not in the Assembly Room. Nor was she anywhere on board. For Penny was one of the three who had died on the mission so far.

*

In no time the room was left with just two occupants: Dugdale, eyes glued to the sweaty, beer-fuelled throwing action of the All-Yorkshire Darts Championship, and Lieutenant Zak Johnston whose attention had been caught by something outside the spaceship. Zak launched himself off a wall and drifted across to the huge panoramic observation window. He peered out, shading his eyes with his hands to cut the glare of the room's fluorescent lights. There was a metal object drifting in space, about two hundred metres from the ship. It was about the size and shape of a large man.

"The Zak-detector's detectin' an inspector," he declared, nose now pressed against the glass.

Dugdale reluctantly shifted his gaze away from the darts and peered past Zak's dreadlocks out of the window. "What the 'ell's that?"

"InspectaBot, that's what."

"Well, what's that mechanical twerk doin' there? 'E should be on t'planet by now, doin' his friggin' job! I launched 'im two hour since."

"Looks lost, dude," said Zak. He raised an arm and waved to the distant robot, but the robot didn't wave back. "Could be inspectin' the view."

"I'll give 'im 'inspectin' t'view'! That clown better get down there an' certify t'base pronto. If I 'ave to spend any more time cooped up on this crock of crap wi' a bunch of lemons, I'll end up batterin' the lot of yer."

"Shoo!" Zak was saying, flapping his arms at the robot to persuade him to go. "Go down to the planet. Start inspecting. Shoo."

Dugdale huffed and puffed as he struggled with his seat belt, but then glimpsed a dart on the screen hitting double-top. His attention returned to the contest. The crowd oohed and aahed as another dart hit its target but the third missed. Flint settled back into his seat. "Get 'im on t'radio and order 'im to get goin'," he said, his eyes firmly back on the screen

Zak looked affronted. "No-can-do, skipperoo. Rest-break. Been promised a cupcake by Lady Emily."

Dugdale grunted. "Well get Lieutenant Willie Walnut to sort out t'mechanical monkey. Tell 'im to order it to gerron wi' its friggin' job! And another thing ..." His voice trailed off as Big Joe "Lard Belly" McGrath stepped up to the oche.

"Sure thing, boss," said Zak. "I'll break my break for the good of the mission. But I ain't missin' the uptake of a cupcake."

3. The Impotence of Being Harnessed

Throughout history, the men and women selected by Fate to make truly remarkable, epoch-making discoveries have not always been the most brilliant of their day: occasionally they have been individuals who might be considered a 'surprise choice'.

Lucy Ugg, for example, a rather formidable, bad-tempered and lice-infested Ethiopian hominid who lived three million years ago. Her ape peers would certainly have considered her a 'surprise choice' for her discovery, had they had the wit to ponder such things. It was she who realized that fire was not just something to run away from but that it had other uses. Such as scorching the furry backsides of her errant offspring, or torching the leafy love-nests of her philandering mate, Toby Ugg. Her greatest discovery, though, had come within the ashes of Toby's final, fatal infidelity. The severe scorching had given her husband a rather delicious crispy crunchy coating. And so, from that simple observation, had been born the barbeque.

Aboard the spaceship *Mayflower III* Fate was about to select Lieutenant Willie Warner as the next 'surprise choice' for a monumental human discovery. As he sat wearing a PredictoHarness in the spaceship's cockpit he hardly looked the part of a great discoverer – an Archimedes, a Kepler, or an Einstein. His was more the look of a man caught up in the webbing of a very uncomfortable high-tech truss. The PredictoHarness, a state-of-the-art exoskeleton, with built-in predictive artificial intelligence, strove to foresee its wearer's every move and 'enhance' it in zero-G. Its principal drawback was that its predictions tended to be wide of the mark and its 'assistance' quite often more of a hindrance than a help. Once inside, it was almost impossible to escape from its clutches as it never occurred to the PredictoHarness that you might want to.

Willie had not donned the harness by choice; his mistake had been to relax and lean back in the cockpit seat, at which point the harness had latched onto its prey and prepared to take over and assist his every move. He wondered what to do. Should he call his crewmate Lieutenant Zak Johnston for assistance, as on all previous occasions? The prospect of the inevitable ridicule did not appeal.

Yet he had to do something; it was dinner time and he was hungry. There was a lunchbox in the refrigerated trunk beneath the cockpit flight desk, but how to get to it without alerting PredictoHarness? He decided to try to outwit it by stealth. Slowly, millimetre by shaky millimetre, he reached his hand towards the lid of the trunk. But the AI exoskeleton was not so easily fooled. In an instant it was aware of his movement and computing probabilities. Within a microsecond it had concluded, with 89% confidence, that Willie wanted to pull up his socks; so, to help, it rammed his arm down towards his ankles.

Locked in this position, Willie considered his options. Call Zak Johnston, or come up with a cunning plan? Still not liking the idea of the former, he focused his mind on the latter. After a few seconds thought, he had it.

With exaggerated movements he pulled up his socks, as though that indeed had been his original intention. PredictoHarness eagerly assisted and then returned him to his starting position. Step 1 successful.

With his other hand he reached towards the flight desk to retrieve a pen. Again, PredictoHarness was only too happy to help. Step 2 done. Then he, accidentally-on-purpose, fumbled the magnetic pen and prodded it towards the cover of the metallic refrigerated trunk. His aim was a little off-target and, for a tense moment, Willie feared it wasn't magnetic enough to latch on to lid of the trunk and would drift off to the far end of the cockpit. But luckily it veered just in time and clamped itself to the lid. Step 3 complete. He casually reached to retrieve it. As PredictoHarness helped him do so, he flicked his wrist at the last second and flipped open the trunk lid. Hey presto, plan achieved.

"Gotcha!" he said as he peered into the trunk, arm still extended. Floating weightlessly inside was a solitary, ultra-slim Tupperware box – the last of the eight-month supply of lunchboxes his mother had lovingly prepared for the journey. He reached for it and, with PredictoHarness's eager help, pulled it out; the exoskeleton even helped him crack open the lid. The aroma that assailed his senses sent him into ecstasy. Not for him the space-junk-food that the other personnel had to endure. This was the business!

He teased out a cheese and piccalilli sandwich and a mini Curly Wurly – his favourite confection, a chocolate-covered caramel ladder. Behind the latter was a little surprise: a photograph of his dog, Boo-Boo. His mum must have slipped it in so that, on the eve of the first human Mars landing, he would be reminded of home.

Holding the picture in one hand, Willie bit into the sandwich, sending a stream of piccalilli into the zero-G atmosphere where it joined a spiralling galaxy of empty crisp packets, crushed beer cans, a banana skin, and thousands of tiny globules of congealed gravy; the detritus left by Mission Commander Flint Dugdale from the previous watch.

Willie stroked the image of Boo-Boo, his only friend, and a powerful wave of homesickness hit him in the gut. A tear beaded in one eye. Mechanically, he reached to wipe the tear away but, for reasons known only to PredictoHarness's unfathomable algorithm, his movement was interpreted as a punch to his own face. Helpfully, the metal clamp around Willie's wrist directed a perfectly placed uppercut to his chin, rendering him instantly unconscious.

*

The warning chime, heralding Willie's imminent epoch-making discovery, cut through the general hum of his dazed brain. Little did he realize that this annoying noise was signalling a profound change in the way humans viewed their place in the Cosmos.

He forced his eyelids open and focused on the fist he had punched himself with. Crushed inside it were the soggy, sticky remains of his half-eaten sandwich. The Curly Wurly and photo of Boo-Boo had drifted away from him, now too far to reach. Indeed, the Curly Wurly was no longer worth reaching having lodged in the outlet of the central heating system where the warm air had reduced it to a flaccid bag of melted chocolate and caramel. Willie felt like crying.

Somewhere in the forest of instrumentation before him and around him, the bleeping continued its incessant call. It had progressed from merely irritating to totally infuriating. He looked about, fuming, searching for the source, ready to smash the device responsible. Having spotted an instrument with a winking light to his left, he then searched for a suitable weapon with which to destroy it. With nothing readily to hand he leaned down and removed the standard-issue space-clog from his right foot. The exoskeleton monitored his movement, calculating probabilities. Eyes fiery red, mouth hissing with rage, Willie raised the clog high, ready to beat the noisy instrument into silence. But that was as far as PredictoHarness let him go. Based on its comprehensive database of human actions it was 73% certain that Willie had removed the space-clog because a small pebble was lodged inside it. Of course, there was always some uncertainty when it came to humans, but 73% was a pretty good bet, so the harness helped Willie vigorously shake the clog to clear it of any foreign matter.

Willie grunted with frustration as the beeping went on and he let the clog float free from his hand. Another idea came to him. With all the guile of his boyhood hero, *Batman*, he reached into his utility belt and pulled out a pair of nail scissors. PredictoHarness perked up, switching to a state of high alertness, ready to monitor the lieutenant's every move. *What's he playing at now?* it wondered, scanning the cockpit eagerly for clues. *The human intends to cut something. But what?* It watched Willie flip the lid of its own central processing unit, grab a bundle of multi-coloured wires and smile cruelly as he held them between the scissor blades. *Got it*, thought the harness and happily helped to squeeze the fingers of its own execution.

As Willie floated gently free of the harness's suddenly limp restraints, he at last became aware of the significance of the irritating bleeping noise. It was coming from the infra-violet detector. A gob of piccalilli, ejected from his sandwich when he had punched himself, had squirted onto the detector's touchscreen, refocusing it on a new section of the Martian surface.

"Blimey O'Reilly," he said, letting out a low whistle. He doggy-paddled through the air to reach the detector, wiped the pickle off the equipment and prodded a button to silence the alarm. His eyes grew wider and wider as he read the results displayed on the screen. The scans of the Martian surface, some 58,000 feet below, had detected something of great significance. "Positive identification at 99% confidence level," was the on-screen message. "Multiple strong, highly-localized, energy-expending anomalies of a non-geological origin, consistent with metabolizing, thermodynamically open chemical systems, highly suggestive of underlying organic mechanisms".

Willie blinked several times. From his astronaut training he knew exactly what that meant. It meant that the infra-violet scanners had detected living creatures on the planet below. More importantly, it meant that the piccalilli from Lieutenant Willie Warner's sandwich had brought about a truly remarkable discovery: he had become the first person to discover Life on Mars.

The question was: what kind of life had Willie just discovered and would it be pleased to see them?

Now read on …

Continue the story in
"The Worst Man on Mars"
by Mark Roman & Corben Duke

Amazon: http://smarturl.it/TWMOM

Website: http://twmom.webnode.com

Acknowledgements

Thanks to Terry Murphy, Maeve Sleibhin, Frank Kusy, Chris Cotterill, Mark Lleonart, and Phil Huddleston for their comments and useful suggestions.

About the Authors

MARK ROMAN is research scientist living in London with his wife and two teenage children. He is still waiting to make a major scientific breakthrough one day.

CORBEN DUKE is a former architect who lives in Dorset with his wife and two dogs. His interests range from archaeology to shed-building.

Mark and Corben have never met. They collaborate entirely by the exchange of e-mails and occasional insults.

Twitter: @MarkRomanAuthor, @CorbenDuke.

E-mail: mark_roman@hotmail.co.uk, corben.duke@gmail.com

GRINNING BANDIT BOOKS

Grinning Bandit Books is an independent publisher that publishes mostly humorous books, including fiction, travel memoirs, and children's book. We currently have 25 books available on Amazon (see below).

Website: http://grinningbandit.webnode.com.

Our books
Fiction

Mrs Maginnes is Dead – Maeve Sleibhin
Five madcap sisters hunt for a dead woman's hidden legacy while having to deal with the police, gypsies, and the old lady's troublesome goat.

Weekend in Weighton – Terry Murphy
First-time private investigator Eddie Greene is having a bad weekend. It's about to get worse.

Scrapyard Blues – Derryl Flynn
Sex, drugs, and rock 'n' roll. How did one crazy night of excess end up with 25 years behind bars?

The Albion – Derryl Flynn
Fast approaching forty, angry, disillusioned and sickened by the mindless violence all around him, Terry Gallagher decides to make good.

The Girl from Ithaca – Cherry Gregory
Neomene of Ithaca, younger sister of Odysseus, reveals what Homer never knew: a woman's view of the Trojan War.

The Walls of Troy – Cherry Gregory
It is seven years into the siege at Troy, and Neomene finds herself defending the Greek camp against fever and Trojan attack. Soon she is embroiled in the destiny of Achilles and the fate of Troy itself.

Flashman and the Sea Wolf – Robert Brightwell
This first book in the Thomas Flashman series covers his adventures with Thomas Cochrane, one of the most extraordinary naval commanders of all time.

Flashman and the Cobra – Robert Brightwell
This book takes Thomas to territory familiar to readers of his nephew's adventures: India, during the second Mahratta war. It also includes an illuminating visit to Paris during the Peace of Amiens in 1802.

Flashman in the Peninsula – Robert Brightwell
Flashman's memoirs offer a unique perspective on the Peninsular War, including new accounts of famous battles as well as incredible incidents and characters almost forgotten by history.

Flashman's Escape – Robert Brightwell
This book covers the second half of Thomas Flashman's experiences in the Peninsular War and follows on from Flashman in the Peninsula.

Short Tails of Cats and other Curious Creatures – Frank Kusy
Fat Buddhists, insomniac cats, wide-boy whales, headless horsemen, Polish plumbers, little piggy home-owners, and partially-sighted mice – something for everyone in this short tale anthology of the absurd.

Science Fiction

Prime: The Summons – Maeve Sleibhin
Despised by her own kind and exiled on a space base, Xai must somehow return home to fulfil her destiny.

Mother and Other Short Science Fiction Stories – Maeve Sleibhin
A collection of science fiction short stories told largely from a female point of view, and range from comic irony to horror.

The Ultimate Inferior Beings – Mark Roman
An ill-chosen spaceship crew encounter a race of loopy aliens and find that the fate of the Universe rests in their less-than-capable hands. Sci-fi comedy.

Travel/humour

Life before Frank: from Cradle to Kibbutz – Frank Kusy
With the young Frank's antics and dodgy dealings driving his poor mother to despair, he vows that one day he will make her proud of him. It is a vow he will find difficult to keep.

Kevin and I in India – Frank Kusy
Two barmy British backpackers take on India in this true story of adventure and misadventure. All Kevin wants is a cheese sandwich...

Rupee Millionaires – Frank Kusy
Want to make a million? Be careful what you wish for ...

Off the Beaten Track – Frank Kusy
What did Frank do to escape the crazy Polish biker chick? He went off the beaten track...

Too Young to be Old – Frank Kusy
When Frank starts working with old people, he rediscovers a young dream. And sets out to India to make it come true.

Dial and Talk Foreign at Once – Frank Kusy
Can Frank cover India for a travel guide in 66 days? Or will he crash and burn?

The Reckless Years: A Marriage made in Chemical Heaven – Frank Kusy
The true story of two people who tried and failed to destroy each other. And fell in love. Again.

Children's Books

Ginger the Gangster Cat – Frank Kusy
Ginger returns from the dead - to carry out the most cunning cat crime of the century. In Barcelona.

Ginger the Buddha Cat – Frank Kusy
Ginger is facing a tough decision. Sausages or enlightenment?

Warwick the Wanderer – Terry Murphy
Rock n' roll: it's the future!

Percy the High-Flying Pig – Cherry Gregory
When Percy the pig decides life on the farm is too boring, he escapes with Sam the sheep dog.